Not having the vaguest idea what he was talking about, Karla frowned at him in confusion. "Scenario? I don't understand. What scenario?"

"The famous artist, beautiful art-gallery-owner scenario," Jared explained.

"What?" Karla stared at him in stunned wonder.

"The famous artist, being me, and the beautiful gallery owner, being you," Jared expanded his explanation, indicating first himself then Karla with one long, lightly haired, strangely elegant index finger. "And the scenario being the love affair I've decided we're going to have."

Love affair? Karla stopped breathing. Love affair! The man was a blithering nut case!

Refusing to acknowledge the sudden acceleration of her pulse rate and the wild thump-thump of her heartbeat, she eyed him warily and took a cautious step back. "I don't have love affairs," Karla said with hard emphasis.

Closing the distance between them with one casual step, he raised her chin with the tip of one long finger. His warm breath misted her lips an instant before his mouth took command of hers...

Joan Hohl

Joan Hohl, a Gemini and an inveterate day-dreamer, says she always has her head in the clouds. An avid reader all her life, she discovered romances about ten years ago. "And as soon as I read one," she confesses, "I was hooked." Now an extremely prolific author, she is thrilled to be getting paid for doing exactly what she loves best.

Other Second Chance at Love books by
Joan Hohl

WINDOW ON YESTERDAY   #450

Watch for

WINDOW ON TOMORROW   #458

coming in March!

Dear Reader:

Second Chance at Love is sure to generate some warmth this January with these two fine selections. You met roommate Karla Janowitz in *Window on Yesterday* (#450), the first of acclaimed author Joan Hohl's trilogy. In *Window on Today* (#454), it's Karla's turn for love—a beautiful tale about two very determined people! And author Kelly Adams incites *Storm and Fire* (#455) when Emma Kendrick meets Joel Rivers, who challenges her with far more than she had bargained for . . .

Karla Janowitz is on top of the world. Her new art gallery is a huge success and her two best friends are in town to help her celebrate. Then, amid the festivities, artist Jared Cradowg shows up, desirous of two things Karla will not yield: one of his paintings—and her heart. But Jared is a man with a vision. He's certain that he and Karla were fated to be together. Powerfully drawn to him despite the inner warnings of her heart, Karla accepts Jared's invitation to an art-inspired tour of Arizona. Against the beautiful background of vast deserts and awesome canyons, they discover their passion for art is far surpassed by their passion for each other. *Window on Today* (#454) is as fulfilling as its prequel. And look for *Window on Tomorrow* (#458), coming in March, when the third of the dynamic trio meets the man of her dreams . . . literally!

Kelly Adams, a master of romantic repartee, will delight you with *Storm and Fire* (#455). Joel Rivers doesn't just disrupt the calm of the day when he calls the Kendrick household, he initiates the first of many surprises. It seems that Emma Kendrick's young nephew has gotten into a bit of trouble at football camp and Joel is all too happy to inform Emma's sister about it. Emma has just one question: Who does this guy think he is? Not only has Joel Rivers punched out her nephew's football coach, but he's also reprimanded her sister and demanded an appearance. Finding herself on an obscure island to fetch her nephew from this ogre's care, Emma is completely unprepared for what awaits. Could this gorgeous, loving father be the same brute on the phone? Emma decides to stick around for a while to find out—and falls in love. Though Joel returns her feelings, he has strong reservations about the future. Can Emma lead him through the storm and fire of his feelings safely—to her?

Also coming from Berkley this month is *Minstrel's Fire* by Anne Harrell. The Minstrel's Rough was the largest uncut diamond in the world—and the most mysterious. Its existence was as legendary as its allure. And no man or woman touched by its beauty could escape the passion, the greed, the dazzling seduction it inspired. Not Juliana Fall, the beautiful and acclaimed pianist who inherited its splendor—and its hidden legacy of danger. Not her esteemed family, who had survived a tragic past because of its brilliant power to entrance. Not the senator who risked his career, and faced the ultimate scandal, to claim its secret value. Nor the Nazi collaborator who would do anything to possess it. No one would ever be the same. *Minstrel's Fire*—a dazzling, fast-paced novel that gleams with danger, romance, and suspense.

And from award-winning author Karen Harper comes a splendid new novel of pride and passion, *Tame the Wind*. Scandal ravaged the halls of King Henry VIII's court, unleashing a bloody turmoil of jealousy and deceit. And yet, in the powerful arms of Captain Edward Clinton, Lady Gera was prepared to cast aside her fears . . . to surrender to his virile charms, his searing kiss, his sensual demands . . . though to do so was the ultimate peril. For Gera was a defiant Irish patriot sworn to revenge. And her beloved Edward had promised his heart and soul to another woman . . . Don't miss this lush historical romance by the author of *One Fervent Fire*.

Finally, a dazzling epic from bestselling author Elizabeth Kary, who brought us *Love, Honor and Betray* and *Let No Man Divide*. *From This Day Onward* weaves a vast American tapestry of love and war, filled with the colorful events and brave men and women who changed the course of history. Meet Jillian Walsh, a Yankee widow who falls for an escaped Confederate prisoner and Ryder Bingham, whose need to avenge his brother's death is as strong as his need for Jillian's love.

As always, happy reading!

Sincerely,

Hillary Cige

Hillary Cige, Editor
SECOND CHANCE AT LOVE
The Berkley Publishing Group
200 Madison Avenue
New York, NY 10016

SECOND CHANCE AT LOVE™

JOAN HOHL
WINDOW ON TODAY

BERKLEY BOOKS, NEW YORK

WINDOW ON TODAY

First edition published January 1989

ISBN: 0-425-11200-4

"Second Chance at Love" and the butterfly emblem are trademarks belonging to Jove Publications, Inc. The name "BERKLEY" and the "B"
logo are trademarks belonging to Berkley Publishing Corporation.

Second Chance at Love books are published by
The Berkley Publishing Group
200 Madison Avenue, New York, NY 10016

Printed in the United States of America

10 9 8 7 6 5 4 3 2 1

WINDOW ON TODAY

CHAPTER ONE

HE STOOD OUT in the chattering crush of art fanciers like a redwood in a stand of scrub pines.

The comparison struck Karla the instant she saw him. His solid-looking height was not the only feature of his appearance to strike her stunned senses.

Carefully setting her wineglass aside, Karla murmured a distracted word of apology and moved away from the middle-aged couple with whom she had been discussing the vitality and appeal of modern American western art.

Although the redwood posing as a man appeared to be the embodiment of every concept she harbored about western art, it was more than his tall, rugged-looking strength that commanded Karla's undivided attention.

He stood aloof and alone in the midst of the crowded

1

gallery. The slanting rays from the westering Arizona sun streamed through the plate-glass window, bathing his deeply tanned skin in a shower of bronze. His gaze was riveted on the large, unframed, attention-grabbing canvas that hung alone in the center of one wall in the main exhibition room.

The oversized portrait was done in oil, in bold colors applied in even bolder strokes. It depicted an Apache Indian, attired in the garb of the working cowboy and mounted bareback on a powerful horse.

Except for his contemporary sartorial trappings—and his lack of a horse—the man staring so intently at the portrait might well have been staring into a mirror.

Recognition caused a shiver to dance along Karla's spine. Without a speck of doubt, she knew the man's identity. Oblivious of the excited hum of conversation around her, Karla wended a path through the throng to the man's side.

"Mr. Cradowg?" Karla's coolly professional tone revealed nothing of the thrilling sense of anticipation and near awe she was feeling.

"Where did you get it?"

Though she flinched inwardly at the cold harshness of his tone, Karla refused to acknowledge or even admit to feeling intimidated by his abrupt question. Reflexively curling her slim fingers into her soft palms, she set her chin at a determined angle and curved her lips into a small smile.

"I didn't realize it was a self-portrait." Her gaze shifted from his hatchet-hewn features to the similar features captured in oil on the canvas.

"It isn't a self-portrait." His expression didn't alter by a flicker. His voice remained detached, his tone implacable. "Where did you get it?" he repeated.

Annoyance flared inside Karla at the imperious sound of his voice, and a shiver of a different emotion coursed through her. She didn't think to ask him how he knew she was the owner of the new art gallery; she merely accepted as fact that he did know. "I found that painting under a stack of reproductions at a church bazaar. Obviously, the previous owner had no idea of its value. I got it for a pittance." Karla also didn't question the tiny thrill of satisfaction she derived from telling him the truth.

Her satisfaction proved unequal to the fiery gaze he turned on her. An untamed and savage light lurked within the depths of his glittering black eyes. Suppressing an unreasonable urge to raise her hand to protect her exposed throat, she gouged tiny crescents into the skin of her palms with her nails. Enduring that chilling black stare was one of the most difficult tasks Karla had ever set for herself.

"I want it." His black stare pierced her composure.

Fury rushed to her rescue, allowing Karla the strength to repair the breach in her armor. "It's not for sale." She moved her head a fraction with rigidly controlled impatience to indicate the discreet Not for Sale tag taped to the wall directly below the canvas.

Except for a tightening along the line of his jaw, his expression remained closed, unrevealing, and more than a little frightening. Beginning to quail, Karla might have agreed to give him anything he wanted if he hadn't, at that moment, muttered something indiscernible, inspiring a shot of steel resolve into her weakening spine.

"It's not for sale," she repeated in a tone of angry constraint.

The smile that curled his lips was insulting; the six-figure purchase offer that hissed through those curling lips was mind-blowing.

Karla couldn't afford to reject his offer, regardless of how offensively it was presented. She had plunged deep into debt to obtain, stock, and open the small gallery in Sedona. She was painfully cognizant of the fact that she could free herself from indebtedness by accepting his offer. She was even more acutely aware of his smug smile as she shifted her glance between him and the portrait. Nevertheless, quivering with satisfaction, she turned him down, enunciating each word succinctly.

"I'm sorry. It is not for sale."

"Anger" was too insipid a word to describe his reaction; even "fury" was too mild a term. Sheer unadulterated rage blazed from his obsidian eyes. Expecting a searing blast when his lips moved, Karla prudently stepped back. In truth, she should have run, for he lashed her with a tongue that dripped frozen acid.

"Somewhat stubborn, aren't you?" His sneer revealed hard teeth that flashed frost white in contrast to his teak-brown tan. "All right." His eyes narrowed. "You want to haggle over price, we'll haggle," he said, returning his drilling stare to her eyes. "But not now." His gaze released her momentarily to sweep the gathering in the small gallery. "I'll be back when we can haggle in private." Refusing her the opportunity to accept, reject, or respond in any way, he whirled around and strode from the gallery.

"Karla?"

In a state of shock and apprehension, Karla barely

recognized her young assistant's voice, or even her own name until it was anxiously repeated.

"Karla?"

Shuddering into awareness, Karla blinked and focused on the young woman's perplexed expression. "Yes, what is it?" she asked distractedly.

"Are you all right?" An odd frown creased her assistant's smooth brow.

Karla forced her stiff lips into a reasonable facsimile of a smile. "Yes, of course, Anne," she said with an assurance she was light-years away from feeling. "Is there a problem?"

The diminutive woman shook her head vigorously. "No, no problem. There are . . ." She broke off to stare at the doorway. "That was Jared Cradowg, wasn't it?" she asked in a tone every bit as oddly strained as her frown.

"Yes," Karla replied tightly.

"I don't believe it! *The* Jared Cradowg!" Anne's eyes grew round as quarters as she swung her gaze to the large canvas. "The very same Jared Cradowg who painted the portrait practically every person here has offered to buy?"

"Yes, the very same." Karla was forced to push the reply through her gritted teeth.

"Holy sh—" Anne caught back the crude word just in time, glancing around frantically to see if she'd been overheard by the patrons standing nearby.

Rattled by the artist under discussion more than she cared to admit, even to herself, Karla held on to her patience and her even tone of voice. "You were about to tell me something," she prodded.

Anne moved her head in a vague little nod. "Yes, but, my God, Jared Cradowg!"

Interpreting the younger woman's reaction as near adulation for the artist, Karla felt her patience shatter, and her voice carried the jagged edges. "Anne, really! Jared Cradowg may be a famous painter, but he's just a man all the same." And a thoroughly unpleasant man at that, she added to herself. "Now, if you could possibly bring your attention to the business at hand, will you get on with whatever it was you wanted to tell me?" Karla's uncharacteristic display of exasperation finally penetrated the younger woman's bemusement.

"Oh!" Anne blurted out, flushing under the fierce frown on her employer's face. "I'm sorry. There are some people who'd like a word with you." She flicked her hand absently toward the far corner of the room.

Karla's gaze followed the indicated direction, and her eyes widened with surprise and delight. Two women and one man stood in the distant corner, and as Karla's wide-eyed gaze settled on them, they raised their glasses in unison in a silent salute to her.

"I don't believe it!" Karla said in a whisper, unconsciously echoing Anne's exclamation of moments before. Her expression bemused, she began walking quickly toward the grinning trio. "I simply don't believe it!"

Amazement and laughter banished the unsettling image of the rough-hewn and even rougher-voiced painter from her mind. Delighted, she strode into the trio and was immediately caught up in a four-way hugging party. The instant they drew apart, four voices began speaking and blending.

"When I sent out the invitations for the opening, I

didn't dream, or dare to hope, any one of you would come, let alone all of you!"

"Miss your opening?"

"Are you kidding?"

"We wouldn't have missed this for anything!"

Karla blinked against the hot sting of tears, and managed a shaky laugh as her gaze devoured the three smiling faces, in which two pairs of eyes were suspiciously bright. The two women were closer to Karla than her own sister, who had sent her good wishes for the opening, but also her regrets. Karla had shared an apartment with these women during the four years of her delayed college sojourn.

"When did you arrive in Sedona?" Karla glanced from one to the other.

"About an hour ago." The response came from Andrea Trask, the woman Karla had dubbed "the innocent one" early on in their acquaintance. "We checked into the motel, then came directly here."

"We?" Karla glanced at the other woman and the man at her side. "But I thought you two were living in Philadelphia," she swung her gaze back to Andrea. "And the last I heard, you were in California."

"Yes," Alycia Halloran—née Matlock—replied, slanting a smile at her husband of six months. "This wonderful man made the flight arrangements, and we landed in Phoenix thirteen minutes before Andrea arrived. We had to run to her gate to be there when she deplaned."

The wonderful man was the renowned historian and author, Sean Halloran, whom Alycia had met when he'd been invited to do a series of lectures at the small eastern Pennsylvania college the women attended.

"My organizational abilities never fail to impress
my adorably unorganized wife," Sean observed dryly.
He draped an arm casually around Alycia's shoulders
and grunted when she poked her elbow into his rib
cage.

All the angry tension the irascible painter had generated drained from Karla and she smiled like a complacent idiot, slipping easily into the camaraderie the four
of them had enjoyed during the weeks preceding graduation and Alycia's and Sean's wedding the previous
spring.

"You really have an excellent turnout, Karla," Andrea observed, glancing around. "This is some crush."

Karla's smile softened as she gazed at the dreamy-
eyed young woman she had watched over like a mother
hen throughout their four years of college. "Yes," she
agreed. "I'm more than gratified by the response, especially considering the number of art galleries there are in
this town."

"Only you, Karla," Alycia inserted on a soft chuckle.

Her smile giving way to a frown, Karla shifted her
attention to Alycia. "Only me—what?"

Alycia's lips curved into a teasing grin. "Only you
would launch a career in a city already bursting with
the same kind of business." Understanding and affection glowed from her soft brown eyes. "You always
need to test yourself by doing something the hard
way."

Karla shrugged and joined in with her friend's
compassionate laughter. But Alycia's remark reminded
her of what she was supposed to be doing. "And at
this moment, I should be testing myself by mingling
with my guests." She skimmed her glance over the
crowd, and grinned when her eyes returned to her

dearest friends. "So, if you three yo-yos will excuse me, I'll mingle, and try to charm a healthy number of my guests into purchasing the merchandise on offer."

"We can help," Andrea said eagerly, turning to her companions. "Can't we?"

"Of course we can, and will." Alycia gave a determined nod of her head. "Is there anything in particular you'd like us to do, Karla?"

Karla had to swallow to clear the emotion from her throat before she could answer. She also turned to glance around the room—and blink the mist from her eyes. When she turned back to them, her smile only wobbled a teeny bit. "The place is littered with empty wineglasses and half-eaten canapés. If you wouldn't mind, you could collect the debris. It would save cleaning-up time when this is over and allow us to get out of here that much sooner." Karla paused, then glanced anxiously from one to the other. "You all were planning to have a late dinner with me—weren't you?"

"Oh, Karla, really!" Andrea exclaimed.

"Which means . . . will you get real?" Alycia laughingly interpreted. "Of course we were planning on taking you to dinner. We have six months to catch up on." She waved her hand to shoo Karla away. "You go to work. Andrea and I will make short shift of the trash, and"—Alycia smiled sweetly at her husband—"Sean will also mingle . . . and very casually mention exactly *who* he is and how very impressed he is with the excellence of the work displayed *and* with the charm of his hostess." She fluttered her eyelashes to the accompaniment of her friends' muffled laughter. "Won't you, darling?"

"Naturally." Sean drew himself up to his commanding height of six feet four inches. His composed features visibly fought the grin that twitched the corners of his lips. "I are famous, you know?" He arched one rust-shaded eyebrow imperiously.

"What you are is crazy," Karla said, choking back laughter.

"That, too," Sean said agreeably, shrugging his wide shoulders.

"Shall we get on with it?" Andrea inserted. "If you two get into one of your comedy routines, you'll never make a sale, Karla." She pulled her expression into stern lines, which was one mean feat for her gentle-looking features. "Get busy, Karla, and make damn sure you pass your test."

Muttering, "Yes, Mother," Karla moved away to be swallowed within the ranks of the chattering crowd.

Her friends knew her well, Karla mused, while managing to converse intelligently with several of her guests. Alycia and Andrea even better than Sean. When space was mutually shared, no matter how spacious the space, it was practically impossible not to know one another. But, Karla reflected, if they knew her, she knew them as well.

Strangely, it had not been their mutual study interests that had drawn the three women together early on in their freshman year of college four years before. In fact, their interests were very diverse.

Alycia was a history major, and admittedly steeped in the past.

Andrea had taken courses in space and nature sciences, and dreamed of playing a role in manned and unmanned space probes in the future.

Of the three, Karla had her feet planted most firmly in the present. She was definitely a woman of her time, a complex combination of soft femininity and self-willed aggression, vulnerable in her confidence, her strength tempered with flexibility. She had passionately wanted to be an artist, but had come to the realization that passion did not necessarily translate into natural talent and that her work would never be more than adequate. Her flexibility and confidence had allowed her to switch gears in midterm of her junior year and set her sights on a different goal—that of displaying and selling the works of gifted contemporary artists and artisans from the region whose art she admired most, the American West.

There were times, many in number, when Karla had yearned to pick up a brush and give painting one more shot. On several of those occasions she had actually gone as far as to drag her art supplies from where she had buried them at the back of a closet, only to shove them away again moments later without even unpacking them.

Unlike many men and women, Karla knew herself quite well. She recognized her limitations and knew her strengths. She faced the world without flinching, very simply because she faced the world, and every soul in it, without pretense or affectation.

Since graduating from college the previous spring, Karla had literally lived her life on the run, first scouting out the perfect location in which to open her gallery, then coaxing, cajoling, and even begging artists and craftsmen to allow her to display their work in the small but elegant building she'd acquired in Sedona, Arizona. She had driven herself a hundred times harder than any legendary task master, and she had driven herself deeply into debt. And all her work, all the haggling, and all the indebtedness had been in preparation for this night, this long yearned for, long feared opening night of her very own gallery, which she had appropriately christened Today's West.

Still ruminating, Karla excused herself from one small but enthusiastic cluster of people to drift away and mingle with others. While she was meandering, her glance repeatedly returned to the riveting, imposing, and brilliantly executed portrait in the center of the wall.

The likeness between the artist and his subject was so incredible that Karla questioned the veracity of Jared Cradowg's claim that the work was not a self-portrait.

The features were the same: broad forehead; long, blade-thin nose; high, jutting cheekbones; squared, thrusting jaw. The hair was black-black, with the sheen of moonlight gliding over rippling, inky waters. The eyes were dark and glittering with unrelenting male defiance. The lips were perfectly shaped, but thin and unforgiving.

Staring at the canvas, Karla had a memory flashback of the day she had discovered it.

She hadn't looked forward to going to the bazaar the month before; she had felt tired and had longed to sleep in that Saturday morning. But she had promised Anne, who was a member of the church that was holding the fund-raising sale. And so Karla had forced an interested expression onto her face and duly trailed her new assistant around the church basement, perusing the handmade crafts and homemade baked goods on sale. Her interest had perked somewhat when they stopped to glance over a small table with a display of miniatures, but immediately noting the lack of quality in the tiny paintings, Karla had transferred her attention to the stack of reproductions propped against one table leg. She was merely biding her time, waiting for Anne, as she negligently flipped through the paintings. An uncanny sensation, not unlike an electric shock, charged through her arm the instant her fingers touched the oversize canvas. The minute she moved the stack forward for a better look, Karla knew exactly what she had found.

Gazing at the portrait, Karla again experienced the thrill and excitement of discovery she had felt that morning, and again shivered from the same joy of ownership she'd felt after purchasing the canvas. She, Karla Janowitz, possessed an original Jared Cradowg painting. What a pity the man appeared unworthy of the enormous talent he possessed.

The thought brought an image of the man and an echo of his promise, or threat, to return to the gallery. Suppressing a shiver, Karla drew her gaze from the portrait and smiled brightly as she turned to yet another group of guests.

What seemed like aeons later, her feet aching in protest against the spike heels on her strappy sandals, Karla stood, ignoring the aches, laughing and conversing with the eager and receptive western art lovers who had so graciously responded to the invitations she had laboriously painted in the glow of a lamp at midnight.

The stated closing hour of nine came and passed, and still the guests lingered, laughing, talking, and buying. Karla was tired to the point of numbness; satisfaction activated the adrenaline that surged through her body, keeping her upright and animated.

As the hour of ten approached, the guests slowly began to decrease in number. Arrangements were made to package and ship, package and deliver, package and hold for pickup. Finally, Karla ushered the last reluctant-to-leave patron from the gallery. After shutting and locking the door, she slumped wearily against it and closed her eyes. Though the room was in hushed silence, she was aware of the eyes of her friends and her young assistant upon her. As she slowly raised her shadowed eyelids, a triumphant smile lit up her face.

"As objective observers," she said, skimming her gaze over the watchful faces, "would you agree that the opening was a resounding success?"

There was an instant of silence; then Karla was pulled away from the door by her laughing friends, to be hugged, kissed, and congratulated.

"It was fantastic, Karla!" Andrea exclaimed.

"*You're* fantastic, Karla," Alycia laughingly corrected Andrea.

"I'm profoundly impressed," Sean said sincerely.

"And I feel privileged to be a small part of it," Anne said softly.

Karla gave her assistant a look of surprise. "A small part?" She shook her head sharply. "Anne! You have worked like a Trojan helping me to get this all together." She hugged the small woman without embarrassment. "And now it's time to celebrate," she announced as she stepped back. She quickly made the introductions she had neglected to make earlier. When the flurry of "How do you do" and "Nice to meet you" was over, Karla glanced around the room and made a face. "We can finish whatever needs to be done tomorrow," she told Anne decisively. "Let's go to dinner."

"Dinner?" Anne repeated, gazing at Karla as if she'd

just suggested they dance naked in the streets.

"Yes, dinner," Karla said. "You know, food, drink, conversation, relaxation?"

Though she smiled, Anne shook her head vigorously. "Not me. I'm too tired to even think about food . . . or any of those other things. All I want to do is go home and drop into bed."

Sean heaved an exaggerated sigh. "These young people just can't keep up the pace. What's this world coming to?"

Rolling her eyes, Alycia smiled at Anne. "Don't mind him, he has a flair for the dramatic. Can we drop you somewhere?"

"No, thank you." Anne returned the smile. "I have my own car." She hesitated, then leaned closer to Alycia and spoke in a stage whisper. "Dramatic or not, I think your husband is as handsome and imposing as Jared Cradowg."

"Thank you." Sean's face was a study in amused confusion. "I think. But who is—" That was as far as Karla allowed him to go before interrupting.

"Am I the only one who's starving?" she cried in a voice that sounded slightly strangled. "Anne, good night. We're leaving—if you don't mind locking up?"

Anne gave her employer an odd look, but readily agreed. "Not at all. I'll see you in the morning."

"Right." Making believe she was unaware of the baffled expressions on the faces of her friends, Karla collected her purse and three-quarter-length cape. Heading purposefully for the door, she called, "Let's move out, troops, I'm famished."

"All right, Karla, tell all," Alycia demanded, in the same teasing manner the three women had exacted information from one another while sharing an apartment. "Who, exactly, is Jared Cradowg?"

They were seated at a round table in one of the finest steak house restaurants in Sedona. The decor was underplayed elegance, and the ambience was relaxing. The conversation from the other late diners in the intimate room was pleasantly muted. Feeling trapped, Karla took a sip of her champagne cocktail and considered how to reply.

"He's no one, really." Her voice and shrug were casual—too casual; her friends were immediately suspicious.

"A friend?" Andrea said teasingly.

"A male friend?" Alycia inquired hopefully.

"A lover?" Sean asked bluntly.

Karla choked on her drink. "Lover!" She sputtered. "Jared Cradowg?" She shuddered. "The man's a throwback to the Stone Age!"

"Really?"

"Indeed?"

"Interesting."

Karla glared at the three grinning faces. "Yes, really. And, yes, indeed. And, no, not interesting."

"Uh-huh."

"Certainly."

"Bull."

Karla eyed her three tormentors balefully and took a cautious sip of her drink. She was well and truly trapped. Without a shred of doubt, she knew they'd tease her unmercifully until she told them who Jared Cradowg was. Karla was mildly surprised that none of the three had recognized his name, especially Sean, who possessed a keen appreciation of western art. As if he'd read Karla's thoughts, Sean suddenly snapped his fingers.

"Cradowg." He repeated the name softly. "Spelled C-r-a-d-o-w-g—but pronounced 'Craddock' . . . right?"

"Yes," she admitted tightly.

"The painter?"

Karla sighed in defeat. "Yes, Jared Cradowg, the painter."

"Is he famous?" Andrea asked.

"Now that you've cleared up the spelling and pronunciation, I do remember the name," Alycia said, turning to her husband.

"Wait a minute." Sean narrowed his eyes thoughtfully. "That large painting of the Apache Indian," he said in a musing tone. "It's a Cradowg, isn't it?"

"Yes," Karla admitted.

"And you were talking to a man right before Anne told you we were at the gallery," Sean recalled aloud. "Was that chiseled giant Jared Cradowg?"

"Yes."

"You mean that deeply tanned hunk?" Andrea asked, eyes widening.

"Yes."

"The one whose face appeared to be chipped from the side of a cliff?" Alycia said in a tone of wonder.

"Yes!" Karla clapped her hand over her mouth and glanced around guiltily. "Yes, yes, yes," she chanted softly. "Now, will you please drop it?"

"Drop it?" Andrea frowned.

"Are you kidding?" Alycia arched her dark eyebrows.

"Why are you so uptight?" Sean asked silkily.

"I'm not uptight." Karla lifted her chin.

"Uh-huh."

"Certainly."

"Ditto."

Karla laughed. She couldn't help herself; it was all so familiar. Even being badgered by them felt good. "I honestly don't know the man." She held up a hand, palm out, to stave off another round of one-word barbs. "Tonight was the first time I ever laid eyes on him," she explained. "And I couldn't have talked to him more than ten minutes."

"I don't think I understand." Andrea frowned again.

"Don't feel like the Lone Ranger," Alycia muttered.

"He must have made some impression," Sean observed shrewdly.

"Yes, he did. He annoyed the hell out of me," Karla confessed. "He was arrogant, rude, and insulting."

Andrea's gentle eyes flashed fire. "What did he say to upset you?"

Alycia's chin angled militantly. "How dare he insult you!"

Sean's back stiffened. "Would you like me to teach him some manners?"

A warm, cared-for feeling spread through Karla, banishing her anger, which had been rekindled by talking about the artist. "No, thank you, Sean, but I appreciate the offer." She smiled wryly. "And 'offer' is the key word." Before she could be bombarded with questions, she quickly explained. "Mr. Cradowg made me an offer for the Apache Indian painting. He became rude and insulting when I refused his offer."

"You own the painting!" Sean was suitably impressed.

Karla laughed. "Yes, I own it. And I have no intention of giving it up, not even to its illustrious and ill-tempered creator." She sighed with relief when she noticed the waiter approaching their table, balancing a loaded tray on the palm of one hand. "Oh, wonderful!" she exclaimed brightly. "I do believe I'm being rescued by the entrée. Do you suppose we could find a topic of conversation during dinner that might be more conducive to digestion?"

The subject of one Jared Cradowg was discreetly dropped. But the man himself was not forgotten, at least not by Karla. Long after she had parted company with her friends, when she was curled into a comfortable position in her bed, the memory of Jared Cradowg's promise to return to the gallery in the morning made her restless with anger . . . and tingly with anticipation.

CHAPTER TWO

"I THOUGHT YOU'D never get here."

Stifling a startled scream, Karla spun around to glare at the man who'd spoken impatiently from directly behind her. The key she had been in the process of inserting into the lock on the gallery door slipped from her trembling fingers and landed on the pavement with a soft jingle.

"Are you trying to give me a heart attack?" she demanded, glaring into his hooded dark eyes. "Or do you just make a habit of sneaking up on people?"

Jared Cradowg's implacable expression didn't change by so much as a flicker. "I didn't sneak up on you," he said in a voice devoid of inflection. "And giving you a heart attack would hardly serve my purpose." A flame flared to life in the depths of his eyes as he raked her slender form with a swift but encompassing glance. "Or anyone else's purposes, either."

The hint of sensuality hidden in his lowered voice caused the tremor in Karla's fingers to skip erratically up her arms, then down through her body. Shocked and angered by her involuntary response to him, she attempted to hide it by returning the insult. Tilting her head defiantly, Karla ran a frosty gaze slowly from the longish gleaming black hair on his well-shaped head down to his expensive but scuffed leather boots six feet and some four or five inches below. As a ploy designed to humiliate, her examination was sadly lacking, for the magnificent male packed into the length of him had a strange effect on her breathing capabilities.

Suddenly inexplicably frightened, Karla stooped to retrieve her keys. Jared moved at the same instant. Their knees bumped; her forehead made contact with his hard chest; their fingers touched directly over the keys.

"Oh!" Karla gasped, then froze, trapped between the solid door and his equally solid body. He didn't move for what seemed like forever but could not have been more than a few seconds. Yet during those seconds, Karla's senses were assailed by the feel, the scent, the essence of him. He was pure, undiluted, 100 percent magnetizing male, and she was shaken by the power radiating from him. "Do you mind?" she asked in an icy tone, raising her challenging gaze to his shadowed, watchful eyes.

"I don't mind at all." A smile teased the corners of his sculpted lips. "As a matter of fact, I'm enjoying this immensely."

Karla gritted her teeth and fought the conflicting urges to slug him or to fling her arms around his neck and bring his face close enough to taste those thin, arrogantly male lips. Amazed at the anticipatory thrill that ricocheted down her spine, she snapped, "Back off!"

He allowed a few more moments to pass with cool deliberation, and only then did he slowly rise and step back. "Nasty little thing in the morning, aren't you?" One nearly straight black brow rose chidingly.

"I'm never nasty." Ignoring his outstretched hand, Karla scooped up the keys before rising with unstudied grace. She favored him with the nastiest smile she could twist her lips into. "And at five feet seven inches, I'm anything but small."

"Honey, anything under six feet is small to me."

Karla stopped breathing altogether for an instant, whether from his use of the casual endearment or from the sexy smile that worked its way over his lips, she didn't know—but then, she really didn't want to know. She covered the pent-up breath that whooshed from her body by spinning around and inserting the key into the lock.

The air inside the showroom was stale with the lingering scent of wine, perfume, and paint. Ignoring the tall man dogging her footsteps, Karla walked to the air-conditioning control on the wall and switched the unit on high. Within moments she could feel the forced air swirling around her, cooler than the late November breeze outside. She turned to face her silent, uninvited customer as she shrugged out of her lightweight suede jacket.

"What are you doing here at nine-thirty in the morning?" Karla made a point of looking at the delicate gold watch encircling her wrist. "The notice on the door clearly states the ten o'clock opening time."

Jared had come to a halt less than a foot from her; his unreadable dark eyes regarded her with nerve-jangling directness. "I told you I'd be back when we could talk in private." His voice was as smooth and deep as a shaded mountain stream; Karla felt the effects of it shimmer from her scalp all the way to her lacquered toenails.

"Haggle," she snapped, furious with him for the sensations she was experiencing. "You said you'd be back to haggle."

He conceded the point with a brief inclination of his head. "And I fully intend to haggle," he drawled. "But the scenario has altered a bit."

Not having the vaguest idea what he was talking about, Karla frowned at him in confusion. "Scenario? I don't understand. What scenario?"

"The famous artist, beautiful art-gallery-owner scenario," he explained in a honey-soft voice.

"What?" Karla stared at him in stunned wonder, more rattled by his sudden display of warm amusement than by his obscure statement.

The lines radiating from the corners of his eyes— lines Karla assumed were the result of squinting in the glare of the Arizona sunlight, certainly not from good humor—crinkled attractively when he laughed. In quick summation, Karla decided his laughter alone should be registered with the authorities as a deadly weapon; the sound of amusement rumbling from his chest had a blowtorch effect on her bloodstream.

"The famous artist, being me, and the beautiful gallery owner, being you," Jared expanded his explanation, indicating first himself then Karla with one long, lightly haired, strangely elegant index finger. "And the scenario being the love affair I've decided we're going to have."

Love affair? Karla again stopped breathing. Love affair! The man was a blithering nut case!

Refusing to acknowledge the sudden acceleration of her pulse rate and the wild thump-thump of her heartbeat, she eyed him warily and took a cautious step back. "I don't have love affairs," she said with hard emphasis.

His gleaming black eyes crinkled again as he noted her cautious retreat. "Good." As it had the night before, his smile revealed strong teeth, blazing white in sharp contrast to his bone-deep tan. "I like my women a little naive."

Karla's spine went rigid with the sense of outrage that seared through her. Damn if the man wasn't a chauvinistic blithering idiot! A sweet, contemptuous smile changed the configuration of Karla's soft lips. "Let me explain, Mr. Cradowg," she began in a tone every bit as sweetly lethal as her smile. "I don't have love affairs because I am *not* naive. Do you get my meaning?" She arched one perfectly shaped eyebrow disdainfully.

"Sure."

The impulse to scream was very hard to resist. Grinding her teeth, Karla wondered how in the world he had managed to infuse so much sexual communication into that one slowly drawn out word. In that instant, she changed her opinion of him. He wasn't a blithering idiot after all; the man was a sexy-as-hell chauvinist! And, of even more concern to Karla, her senses and body were responding to him like a moisture-starved desert blossom unfolding to a reviving mist of rain! In the very next instant, Karla knew she had to get rid of him, get him out of her showroom, and her vicinity, before she made an absolute scatterbrained spectacle out of herself and, in the process, ruined her image of herself as a liberated, savvy, totally today woman.

"Okay," she said, exhaling wearily. "You've had your morning amusement. But I have work to do, so why don't you trot on home and play with your... paints?"

Jared's bark of appreciative laughter ricocheted off the matte-finished walls, then arrowed into the depths of her heart. "I *work* with my paints, darling." Closing the distance between them with one casual step, he raised her chin with the tip of one long finger. While she stared wide-eyed at him, he slowly, slowly lowered his head. "But I'm ready to play whenever you are." His warm breath misted her lips an instant before his mouth took command of hers.

Karla froze, and then she thawed, and then she melted. While her intellect issued a warning to withdraw, Karla pliantly allowed his arms to draw her into a shockingly intimate embrace. And while her sense of self-preservation insisted she cease and desist, Karla eagerly obeyed the request of his probing tongue to open her mouth for him. And while, somewhere on the edge of consciousness, she realized his endearments were uttered because he probably didn't even know her given name, Karla shivered in response to the sweet hot thrust of his tongue.

His lips moving on hers as though he was intent on devouring her with his mouth, Jared murmured a deep-throated growl and slid his broad hands to her neatly rounded bottom. His fingers flexed into the soft flesh, then tightened to draw her up and into the heat of his taut body.

Instead of feeling shocked by the contact with his aroused body, Karla experienced a shattering thrill of acceptance. Her intellect, sense of self-preservation, and conscience obliterated, her very consciousness balancing delicately on the edge of nothingness, she clasped her arms around his corded neck and arched her spine, pressing her tingling breasts to his chest and her quivering hips to the blatant maleness of him. Clinging to him with every ounce of feminine power she possessed, Karla feasted on the taste of Jared's mouth, inhaled the spicy scent of Jared's masculinity, and absorbed the essence of Jared into her soul.

How long the kiss lasted, or would have endured, Karla didn't know, but it ended when the alerting sound of a key being turned in the back door pierced the fog of sensuality clouding her mind. Jared relinquished his claim on her mouth the instant she began to struggle, but though he raised his head, he maintained his hold on her body.

"My assistant!" she gasped, trying, and failing, to escape his embrace. "She'll be walking in in a few moments. Please let me go."

"If you'll agree to have lunch with me," he said calmly, in an outrageous attempt at blackmail.

At that moment Karla would have agreed to almost anything to avoid the embarrassment of having Anne discover her wrapped in Jared's arms, but it was impossible. "I can't," she said in a frantic whisper. "I have an appointment." Truth rang in her tone, simply because she'd told him the truth; Karla had agreed to meet her friends for lunch before they left for Phoenix, where they would catch two planes bound for different directions.

Jared's arms tightened. "Dinner." It was not a question; it was a demand.

Karla cast an anxious look at the door leading to the back office, where Anne was probably hanging up her coat at that minute. "Yes! Now will you let me go?"

"Seven?"

"Whenever!" Karla's voice had a decided edge.

Jared smiled and lowered his head to brush his lips over hers. "All right." He brushed her lips again on his backward motion. "And we will have an affair," he murmured. "Until seven, my sweet—Karla." His arms released her and then, moving with a silent swiftness she wouldn't have believed possible in such a big man, he was gone. The showroom door closed behind him as the office door opened behind Karla.

He knew her name.

The recurring thought distracted Karla at odd moments throughout the morning. Carefully avoiding asking herself why it should be so important to her that Jared had bothered to find out her name, Karla went about her daily routine with outward composure, while inside she was a mass of conflicting emotions, the strongest of which was self-recrimination.

What in sweet heaven had come over her?

The question jabbed at Karla with the painful regularity of a sore tooth. Her responsive capitulation to Jared's advance was so uncharacteristic, so out of sync with her normal behavior, that Karla was left with a residue of confusion and impatience.

Jared Cradowg was a man, like other men, and the fact that she had not merely responded to him but had responded with abandonment was an unpalatable dose of self-knowledge for Karla to swallow.

Well, perhaps Jared wasn't *quite* like other men.

The thought brought Karla up short. Standing as still as if she'd been suddenly turned to stone, she stared out through the gallery window, blind to the magnificence of the panoramic view of the surrounding rock cliffs, blazing red in the morning sunlight. As her probing gaze turned inward, she contemplated the direction her unsettled mind seemed bent on taking.

Why was Jared not quite like other men?

Karla knew the answer to that question—she simply shied away from forming it. Still, her feelings, her emotions, her consciousness, insisted she not only form the answer but examine it, dissect it, face it without flinching.

To the casual observer, even to Anne, who had come to know her as well as she allowed most people to know her, Karla appeared cool, composed, but distracted. Her appearance was a facade she had carefully, painfully erected many years before as a defense.

Inside, where Karla lived, she was beginning to tremble in protest to the answer presenting itself against her will. Her eyes open but narrowed, Karla stared out the window at the appealing modern western city—and confronted old established fears ingrained in her self.

Jared Cradowg was not different from other men merely because he was an exceptionally talented artist, or because he was an extremely attractive man—in an earthy, wholly masculine way. No, the intangible that set Jared apart from other men was the responsive emotion he so effortlessly drew from her. Jared was the cause—Karla was the effect. And it scared the hell out of her.

Karla had traveled the route of personal and emotional cause and effect before. She had paid the price of a destructive relationship in the coin of pride and self-esteem. When finally, emotionally bankrupt, she had walked away from the destructive situation, Karla had determined to avoid at all costs that rock-strewn pathway from involvement to commitment.

At the time, young in years, but old, bitter, and wise

in experience, Karla had laughed in self-mockery while declaring she would commit herself to an institution before she'd commit herself to another man.

Yet now, only a few years later in actual time but light-years in terms of Karla's personal growth, she identified and was terrified by the revitalized juices surging thick and hot through her body in response to Jared Cradowg.

In other words, Karla knew she was in deep trouble in regard to Jared. His appeal was basic in nature; something in him silently communicated to something in her.

"Karla, don't you have a twelve-thirty appointment with your friends for lunch?"

The sound of Anne's voice jarred through Karla, shattering her concentration and dispersing the disruptive quiver attacking her nervous system. Both annoyed and gratified by the interruption, she gathered her thoughts and senses together before turning to reply to her assistant with a brittle smile of composure.

"Yes, I do." Karla shot a quick glance at her wristwatch, and concealed her amazement on discovering the amount of time she had spent on inner scrutiny. "I'd better leave."

"Yes." Anne's smile revealed her confusion, but she refrained from commenting on Karla's distraction.

Grateful for the younger woman's reticence, Karla gave her a warm, genuine smile. "I doubt that I'll be back after lunch. Can you handle it on your own?"

Anne's slight frown was wiped away by her soft laughter. "You've trained me very well, Karla. Yes, I'm sure I can handle it on my own."

Karla flashed a grin as she headed for the back office and her handbag and cape. Within minutes she was behind the wheel of her secondhand car, silently giving thanks for whatever had guided her the day she had decided to hire Anne, who had been eager but inexperienced.

Since her friends were planning to leave directly after lunch, Karla had suggested they meet at the restaurant adjacent to their motel. As she drove onto the parking lot, she felt her breath catch in her throat at the awesome view.

The motel stood close to the edge of a cliff, affording a panoramic view of a section of Oak Creek Canyon. A wry smile curved Karla's lips as she stepped from the car, recalling the awe and trepidation she had felt on her initial trip into Sedona to scout out possibilities for her gallery. As her friends had done, Karla had flown into Phoenix on that hot day in late spring and had rented a car to drive to Sedona. Armed with a map, she had decided to enter Sedona via the scenic route. And scenic had barely described the drive down the cliff face into Oak Creek along a switchback road composed of a series of hairpin curves. The memory of her sweaty palms and amazed senses brought a soft chuckle to Karla's lips.

"Uh-huh, the pressure's gotten to her and she's beginning to unravel. Laughing to oneself is the first sign."

Startled by the dryly voiced observation, Karla whipped around, her chuckle growing into full-throated laughter as she encountered the smiling faces of her friends.

"I agree." Alycia nodded solemnly at Sean. "Do you think we should begin to worry about her?"

"*Begin* to worry!" Andrea piped in. "I thought we'd been worrying for almost six months."

Asking herself if she'd ever get used to being cared

about, Karla blinked the mist of tears from her eyes and managed a shaky smile.

"I was recalling the first day I came here, and my reaction to the scenic drive into Oak Creek Canyon," she explained, linking her arms through Alycia's and Andrea's.

"Aha! That explains it then." Sean looked relieved, which obviously hadn't been easy, considering the gleam of humor in his eyes. "Karla isn't going around the bend. She was merely reliving an experience that was similar to the one the three of us shared yesterday."

Karla tilted her head to look up at him. "You drove into Sedona via the scenic route, too?"

Sean nodded. "I loved it." He grinned. "At least what I could see of it while negotiating those curves."

"It was fantastic!" Andrea agreed enthusiastically.

"It was absolutely terrifying!" Alycia shuddered. "I was numb with fear and barely breathing by the time we finally got to the bottom."

Feeling the reflexive quiver in the slender arm linked through hers, Karla frowned at Alycia. "I didn't know you had a fear of heights."

Alycia's smile was weak. "I suffer from acrophobia with a capital A. I have since I was a child." Her eyes grew shadowed with a faraway, dreamy expression. "I think it has something to do with being thrown from a horse during a previous incarnation." Her voice held the tone of utter conviction.

Andrea nodded in solemn agreement. "Of course, that would explain it."

Karla came to an abrupt stop and rolled her eyes in Sean's direction, as if beseeching help. "Please, don't start that reincarnation hocus-pocus again," she pleaded, referring to the esoteric belief held by both of her friends.

Alycia's smile was soft with understanding. "You really do have difficulty with the concept of reincarnation, don't you?"

"Oh, no." Karla shook her head in sharp denial. "I have difficulty with the freeway—any freeway. I have difficulty balancing my financial accounts. I have difficulty allocating my time so as to fit all of my activities into the hours available each day." She smiled wryly. "In other words, I have more than enough to cope with in this lifetime, thank you. Spare me the mumbo jumbo about previous existences."

"You don't know the wealth of experience you're missing," Andrea said, smiling but serious.

"Well, what I don't know . . . and all the rest of that old adage," Karla retorted.

"You're totally earthbound," Alycia accused, laughing. "And totally enmeshed in the here and now of today."

"Totally," Karla agreed, laughing with her.

"Which probably precludes even the possibility of believing in UFOs and extraterrestrials, I suppose," Andrea interjected.

Karla nearly choked on her laughter. "You suppose correctly, innocent one." She glanced quizzically at Sean. "What do you think about all this?"

Sean shrugged. "I think your beliefs, or lack of them, are your business." An attractive smile curved his lips. "And since we have less than three hours left before we must leave for Phoenix," he continued, glancing at his wristwatch, "I also think it's time for lunch."

Alycia smiled with smug satisfaction. "Did I marry a diplomat—or what?"

Before either Karla or Andrea could respond, Sean began shepherding the three laughing women toward the motel restaurant. "On that note," he drawled, "I'll end this discussion." He grinned. "Before one of these two decides I am definitely an 'or what.'"

In light of the swiftly approaching time of parting, lunch was a bittersweet delight. The food, though well prepared and delicious, was consumed without much notice. The conversation was animated and centered mainly on the future plans of the four close friends.

"Since I haven't been able to get into NASA," Andrea said, in a bright tone that failed to conceal her disappointment, "I've decided to stay in the San Francisco area and further my studies at Berkeley."

"And since Sean is about ready to begin working on a new historical tome," Alycia piped up, "I've decided to do my postgraduate work at the University of Pennsylvania."

Karla raised her eyebrows at Sean. "Does this mean there are no plans for a little Halloran in the near future?"

Sean's laughter was easy and relaxed. "Not at the moment," he admitted. "But that could change." He smiled intimately at his wife.

Karla got the picture; Sean was telling her, without telling her, that he and Alycia were not taking preventive measures. As she was aware that her friend actually longed for a miniature reproduction of herself and Sean, Karla wished her success, while she herself couldn't imagine coping with either a husband or child, never mind both.

"And you are going to be knocking yourself out to make a smashing success of your gallery . . . right?"

Alycia asked the question they all knew needed no reply.

Karla answered anyway. "Of course." To herself, she added: As soon as I dispatch the disruptive influence of an artist named Cradowg. Then, refusing to acknowledge the feeling of trepidation or the shiver of response she felt at merely thinking his name, Karla launched into a discussion about mutual acquaintances, none of whom she was the least bit interested in. Her evasive tactics protected her throughout the remainder of the meal and their time together.

The feeling of trepidation, with accompanying shivers, crept over Karla once again while she was dressing for the dinner appointment Jared Cradowg had blackmailed her into that morning. Karla understood perfectly that the former sensation was generated by the latter response.

She didn't want to have dinner with Jared; she didn't want to be in the same room with Jared; in all honesty, Karla felt uneasy about being in the same county as Jared Cradowg.

Carefully choosing attire that would project an image of cool professionalism, Karla stepped into a pencil-slim charcoal-gray skirt and tucked in the tails of a tailored pearl-gray silk blouse before closing the zipper and fastening the button on the waistband. After slipping into the tailored suit jacket and a pair of slim-heeled black pumps, she backed away from the full-length door mirror to eye her reflection critically.

She was satisfied with her appearance—from the neck down; the outfit projected the picture she had hoped to achieve—cool, composed, businesslike. But her reflection from the neck up wrenched a sigh from her suddenly tight throat.

In contrast to the severely conservative attire and underplayed makeup, her natural skin tone was tinged with a pearlescent glow and her hazel eyes sparkled from an inner light, the cause of which she absolutely refused to contemplate. But most demoralizing of all was the look of vulnerability, due entirely to the silky strands of dark hair that had escaped the classic knot at the back of her head. The wisps of silk lay in silent invitation against her neck.

Muttering an expletive that contradicted the look of vulnerability, Karla raised her hands and stepped closer to the mirror, determined to redo the hair knot. The sound of the apartment doorbell arrested her hands in midair.

Jared? Already?

For an instant, Karla froze, her tense body seemingly incapable of motion. Then her gaze shot to the face of the small clock on the nightstand by her bed. The clock read 6:51, nine minutes before the stated time. Maybe it wasn't Jared.

The doorbell rang again, a short, sharp summons directed by the jab of an impatient finger.

Karla's soft lips twisted wryly as she slowly lowered her arms. The commanding sound of the bell convinced her it had been Jared's finger doing the jabbing.

Returning her glance to the mirror, she swept her gaze the length of her reflection, sighed again, and then, squaring her shoulders, turned and walked out of her bedroom.

His finger made contact with the doorbell again as Karla crossed the moss-green living room carpet. Gritting her teeth in annoyance, she unlocked the door and swung it open with barely leashed anger. His index finger was ready to make yet another jab at the abused doorbell button.

"Are you deliberately trying to demolish my bell?" she demanded in outrage.

Looking not at all chastised, Jared casually lowered his arm and just as casually grinned at her. "No," he answered in an offhand drawl. "I was deliberately making sure you would answer, not ignore it."

She frowned as she stepped back, allowing him entrance into the apartment. "Why would I ignore it?"

The sound of Jared's laughter skipped down her spine and reactivated her shivers. "To avoid having dinner with me by pretending not to be here, of course," he replied dryly.

Feeling a sinking sensation inside, Karla stared at him, at the masculine attraction of him, and ground her teeth. She hadn't even thought of avoiding him by pretending not to be home.

Why hadn't she thought of it?

CHAPTER THREE

THE QUESTION DISTRACTED Karla while Jared sauntered into the center of the living room and ran his artist's gaze over her decor.

Karla hardly noticed his brief nod and expression of approval of her tasteful blending of earth tones on the walls and draperies and in the carefully selected pieces of furniture. However, she did notice how appealing he looked, and she admired the contrast of his expertly tailored three-piece suit on a rangy frame that seemed more suited to jeans and boots.

"Excellently done. Vivid yet soothing."

Jared's concisely stated opinion shouldn't have affected her in any way, yet it successfully dissipated her distraction and snagged her attention. Karla felt a spark of annoyance at the warm sensation of pleasure that swept over her. She didn't give a rip whether or not he approved of her decorating skills. So why was she standing there blushing like a teenager? The realization that she was blushing—a phenomenon she had not experienced for some years—deepened her annoyance. Resentfully silent, she stared daggers at his broad back and fought for control of her stupid sensibilities.

When she didn't respond, Jared turned to pin her with dark eyes gleaming with amusement. "I can see you're impressed." His appealing mouth quirked into a sardonic smile as one neatly shaped eyebrow lifted in a chiding arch. "You don't really give a damn what I think about your place, do you?"

"Should I?" Karla countered, suppressing a sigh of relief at her minor victory over her involuntary response to his compliment.

"Possibly." He took one step toward her.

"Why?" She took one step back.

Jared's expression enveloped her like a warm spring shower. "The simple fact that our tastes are similar," he explained, taking two long strides.

His move had halved the distance between them, instilling an odd sense of claustrophobia in Karla. Fighting a sensation of incipient panic, yet determined to stand her ground, Karla raised her chin and put a chill into her voice. "In what way are our tastes similar?"

"In the most basic ways." He smiled when she stiffened. "Colors." He moved one hand negligently to indicate the room. "Art genres." He motioned toward the western prints on the walls. "Attraction to the opposite sex." His lips curved into a sexy smile as he ran a devouring glance the length of her tension-taut body.

"Attraction to the . . ." Karla's voice evaporated in the heat searing her throat.

"You deny the mutual attraction?" One more long

step brought him within scenting distance of her quivering nostrils.

"Certainly!" Karla exclaimed, groaning silently at the lack of strength in her voice.

"You're afraid of me." Sheer male satisfaction was woven through his soft voice.

It was true, but Karla would have choked before admitting it. "You delude yourself," she retorted, in what she hoped was a tone of dismissal.

"I think not." In a move calculated to bring his body into contact with hers, Jared took another step.

The light touch at chest and hip created havoc in every nerve ending in Karla's body. Stubbornly refusing to retreat before his sensuous advance, she clenched her fingers and glared at him. "Back off, buster," she said in a gritty snarl.

Jared didn't take offense at her demeaning order, nor did he snap back at her. Without a word or signal of warning, he dipped his head and captured her anger-tight mouth with his warm lips. A shocked gasp parted her lips beneath his. He was quick to grasp the opportunity, slipping his searching tongue into the moist heat of her mouth while molding his lips to hers.

Karla's senses exploded. Electrical impulses danced a shimmering, erratic tattoo from the nape of her neck to her thighs. Stunned by the intensity of her reaction to his prodding mouth and probing tongue, she stood motionless, unresponsive to a command from her dissolving consciousness to end the sweet torment by pushing him away.

She was helpless; she knew it, and she didn't care. For the moment, Karla's entire reality revolved around this man's mouth and tongue and the arms he closed tightly around her.

The restless movement of his hands caressing her back created a static spark from her jacket. Karla felt the tingle transmit itself from the surface of the material through the receptive silk of her blouse, then splinter to spear into her skin like tiny pinpoints of erotic pleasure.

It was unbearable. It was wonderful. She wanted it to stop, and prayed it would never end.

"Where?"

The husky sound of his voice pierced her bemusement, even though the meaning of his one-word question eluded her. Forcing open the eyelids she couldn't recall closing, Karla gazed at him from sensuous cloudy eyes. "What?"

"We can't make love standing here," he said unevenly, the words spaced between tiny, biting kisses. "And since I'm too tall for the couch, I suggest we move to your bedroom. Where is it?"

The words "make love" and "bedroom" hit her with gale-force impact. Karla could feel her eyes growing wider with shocked disbelief. Had she given him evidence of willingness? she wondered vaguely. Of course she had, she acknowledged. Who, if not she, had been and still was pressed to him as securely as if she were attached with Krazy Glue?

Feeling a smothering sense of self-betrayal, Karla slid her encircling arms from his neck to press her palms to the rigid line of his shoulders.

"Let me go . . . please." Her voice crackled from her parched throat.

Jared frowned but released her. "I don't understand. A moment ago, you were like liquid fire in my arms, against my mouth." His tongue flicked over his lips as if collecting the flavor of her. "Why are you so cold now?"

Pure, unadulterated fear. Karla bit back the spontaneous response and drew a deep breath while gathering her
defenses. "I agreed to share a meal with you," she finally answered, shaking her head slowly back and forth
in repudiation. "I didn't agree to share either my bed or
my body."

"Oh, Karla." His voice held a sigh, his smile held a
hint of pity. "Don't you realize that you're attempting to
deny the inevitable?" He brought his hand to her face to
trail the pad of a finger over her cheek and across her
trembling lips.

"No." Karla shook her head to enforce her denial,
and to dislodge his arousing finger. "I don't believe in
the inevitability of anything."

He gave her a tolerant look and stepped back.
"You're wrong, you know. We were fated to be lovers."

The scant inches of breathing space he'd allowed her
gave her the strength to reply with firm conviction.
"Sorry to disillusion you, but I don't believe in fate,
either."

Jared's soft laughter undermined her renewed confidence. "Time will tell, my sweet," he taunted her
gently. "But, for now, shall we go to dinner . . . and ap-
pease one of our natural, inevitable hungers?"

His verbal dart made a direct hit. Against her will,
Karla was forced to accept the inevitability of the body's
craving for food every X number of hours. The undis-
puted fact sent a surge of embarrassed heat to her
cheeks. Jared's laugh of unconcealed delight intensified
her color to a dusky rose. Wheeling away, she grabbed
her cape from the closet and hurried out of the cloying
confines of the apartment. His laughter trailed her to the
car parked in the street in front of her building.

The car was a distracting surprise. For whatever inexplicable reason, Karla would have wagered money she couldn't afford on a bet that Jared drove a large, solid, probably custom-built, wildly expensive car. The vehicle he was in the process of unlocking was large and very solid-looking, but there the comparison ended. And although it had very likely cost a tidy sum, the vehicle was a sporty but rugged-looking four-wheel drive, go-anywhere arrangement of metal painted a gleaming black and silver.

"Practical," she murmured as he handed her into the plushly upholstered bucket passenger seat.

"In all things," he rejoined, swinging the door shut with a thunk. He slid behind the wheel seconds later and continued as smoothly as if there had been no pause, "From the selection of a car to the acceptance of the inevitability of certain potentially explosive attractions."

Karla turned in her seat to give him a level, narrowed look. "Don't start that again." Her voice had a tightly controlled edge of warning.

Jared chose to ignore it. "Why not? I'm finding it a fascinating subject."

Her control broke. "Well, I'm not! So will you please just drop it?"

"Your wish, and all that," he said expansively, slanting a wicked grin at her. "What do you suggest we talk about?"

Karla gritted her teeth. "Would it be beyond your scope to discuss the purpose for this dinner date you blackmailed me into?" she snapped, thinking about the painting he'd promised to haggle over with her.

Jared shifted gears to accommodate the climb up the steep gradient before answering in a soft drawl. "Honey, that was the point of my discussion."

Karla was immediately on guard. "What do you

mean?" she demanded, glancing around suspiciously as he brought the car to a jarring stop. A sigh whispered through her lips as she realized her suspicions were groundless; he had parked the car in a lot adjacent to a restaurant perched on the side of a humpback hill. She swiveled around to face him again at the now too familiar sound of his soft laughter.

"My purpose in blackmailing you into having dinner with me, my sweet," he said easily, "was to convince you of the inevitability of the affair we are about to engage in."

Determined not to betray the shocking shiver of anticipation she was suffering, Karla shrugged and calmly unlatched her seat belt. "Oh, is that all?" she tossed back carelessly. "And here I was, worried you were going to try to talk me into selling that painting to you." His silky voice arrested her hand as she reached for the door release.

"Oh, I plan to acquire the portrait of my grandfather as part of the deal."

Grandfather? Deal? *What?* Karla's mind was racing too fast to allow coherent sentences to gather on her tongue. And while she was immobilized by speculation, Jared was all motion. After stepping from the car, he circled it and pulled her door open.

"I don't know about you, honey," he said briskly, urging her out of her seat, "but I'm starving."

Bemused and confused, Karla permitted him to usher her across the parking lot and into the restaurant. She didn't catch her breath until they had been seated at a secluded corner table by a wide window, and she found herself in possession of an oversize gold-scripted menu. The minute she came to her senses, she decided to end the charade.

"I'm not hungry," she said, setting the menu aside.

"Of course you are," Jared retorted, handing the menu back to her. "And not only for food." He gave her a contemplative look. "I can't help but wonder how long it's been since you've been intimate with a man," he mused, watching her intently.

Forewarned by his expression, Karla was prepared to meet his thrust with a cool parry. "I can't help but wonder how long it's been since you've displayed a modicum of tact." She offered him a cool little smile.

Jared's laughter rumbled from his chest. "Touché, darling. You're a worthy opponent. If I had a glass, I'd raise it."

"You could raise the white flag instead," she suggested in a sugar-coated tone.

"Surrender?" Jared managed to look astounded, even around the grin revealing his white teeth. "Not me, honey. I said you are a worthy opponent; I didn't concede victory."

Karla would have launched an offensive had the waiter not appeared at their table at that moment. Conserving her energy for the next skirmish, she ordered a drink and a meal, and promptly forgot about both. While Jared discussed the merits of the entrées with the waiter, she glanced out the window and felt her breath catch in her throat.

The bright fall moonlight bathed the landscape in a silvery glow and cast the jutting rocks and cliffs into stark relief. Below the restaurant, gold lights twinkled from homes and street lamps, lending the scene a fairyland aura.

"Pretty, hmm?"

"Beautiful," Karla replied, relinquishing one spectacular sight for another, as she turned to gaze into Jared's dark eyes. "I'm continually thrilled by the splendor of the rocks and cliffs of this canyon."

"It is pretty impressive. Nothing like the Grand, of course." Jared shrugged.

"I wouldn't know," Karla admitted. "I've never seen the Grand Canyon."

"Never seen it?" he repeated, frowning. "How long have you been in Arizona?"

"Not quite six months. I came to Sedona to look around for a location to open my gallery in late May, a week after graduation," she explained.

Jared looked puzzled and was about to ask a question when the waiter arrived at their table with their drinks. He drummed his fingers lightly on the tabletop until the waiter served the drinks, along with a condiment tray, and departed.

"Graduation?" His eyebrows arched. "Graduation from what?"

Karla's smile was wry. "College."

The puzzled expression remained on his face. "You were working for your master's?"

She sighed. "No, I was working for my bachelor's degree." His sharpened gaze probed her face, and anticipating his question, Karla answered it before he could ask. "Due to circumstances, I began college a little later than most people do."

"What circumstances?" Jared fired the question at her the instant she finished speaking.

Telling herself she should have known he'd demand a fuller explanation, Karla toyed with the stem of her glass, while carefully considering her reply. Her personal life was really none of Jared Cradowg's business and . . . Her thought train derailed as she became aware of the sensation of cold moisture against her fingertips.

Curious, Karla glanced down at the glass, her eyebrows drawing together as she stared in disbelief at the frothy contents.

Had she actually ordered the margarita? she asked herself in amazement. Though it was true that occasionally Karla thoroughly enjoyed the flavor of the pale lime-flavored concoction, she was well aware of the potency of the tequila mixture, and its potential for loosening the tongue and relaxing inhibitions.

Scowling at the innocent-looking icy bomb, Karla reflected that the absolute last thing she needed while in Jared's company was a stimulant containing the power to relax her inhibitions. Warning herself to keep her thoughts together, she raised the glass to her lips and took a tentative sip.

"What circumstances?"

Karla winced at the rough impatience edging Jared's low voice, and covered the reflex by touching the tip of her tongue to the salt-encrusted rim of the glass. The salt lodged in the gasp that caught in her throat when she glanced up to encounter his smoldering gaze riveted to her mouth.

"Ah . . . umm . . . ahem." Karla was forced to take a sip from her water glass to ease the sting at the back of her throat. "I . . . ah, that is . . ." A low growl from Jared put an end to her inane attempt at speech.

"Don't do that again."

Karla started in surprise. "That? What?" She shook her head, dislodging several silky strands of dark hair, which settled like wispy feathers against her neck. "Don't do what again?"

Jared groaned. "Either or."

Baffled, and completely unaware that she continued to hold the margarita in one hand and the glass of water in the other, Karla exclaimed, "Either or what?"

His expression an odd combination of exasperation and amusement, Jared reached across the table to relieve her of the glasses and set them on the table. "I'm beginning to suspect that you might be a trifle flaky," he observed dryly.

"Flaky!" Karla bristled. "Me? I? What do you mean?"

Jared's mouth quirked into a teasing smile. "I only mean . . ." He broke off as he caught sight of the waiter, large tray balanced on one palm, approaching their table. "Forget it. Here's our dinner."

Forget it! Karla repeated to herself. Ha! There was no way she'd forget it. She certainly was not the least bit *flaky*, and she had every intention of setting Mr. Bigtime Artist straight on that score the minute the waiter removed himself.

Suddenly as parched as if she had flung the angry spate at him aloud, Karla grasped a glass and drank thirstily. Unfortunately, the glass contained the icy margarita.

"Going at it a little strong . . . aren't you?" Jared was unsuccessful at controlling the twitch of amusement tilting his lips.

Karla glared at him. "That's my business—and I'm not at all flaky!"

Jared choked back a burst of laughter, which was wise, as Karla would very likely have flung the remainder of the drink at him. Correctly reading her mood, he locked his features into a somber mask.

"Yes, I understand," he said in a gentling, soothing tone.

"And don't patronize me!"

He lost the inner battle; the laughter erupted, but his

long fingers curled around her wrist before she reacted by showering him with the cold liquid. "You do have a temper," he said mildly, applying pressure on her wrist until she was forced to set the glass on the frilly cocktail napkin. Then he waited, with obvious deliberation, until she released her grip on the glass, before continuing. "So do I," he murmured in a tone meant to reach only as far as her ears. "We're going to be great together, in and out of bed."

Growing stiff with outrage, Karla raked her mind for a crushing reply. Her rattled brain wasn't quick enough; Jared effectively defused her anger with a blandly voiced query.

"Don't you think we had better eat our food while it's still reasonably warm?"

Distracted, Karla blinked and lowered her gaze to the large dinner plate the waiter had set before her. Good grief! she moaned inwardly. What had possessed her to order so much food? In a strange state of fascination, she took silent inventory of the plate: prime rib, end cut, awash in its own juices; baked potato, extra large, drenched in butter and sour cream; asparagus, thick, white, six spears, dressed in a Cheddar cheese sauce. Karla did a swift computation of calories and groaned aloud.

Jared frowned. "It isn't what you ordered?"

How should I know? Karla thought—but prudently kept the question to herself. "Er . . . I had no idea the portions would be so large," she improvised. "I never eat this much food at one sitting."

He ran a comprehensive glance over her torso. "I believe you." His shrug was casual. "So eat what you like and leave the rest."

Karla detested food waste, but under the circumstances, she was left with little choice. Since she had, however unconsciously, created the situation, she accepted it with a sigh, and draped her napkin over her lap.

The flow of conversation was slow and awkward as they began the meal, and Karla started out by picking at her food. Then, gradually, the tempo increased, in both consumption and communication, and she found herself enjoying every morsel she popped into her mouth. Jared asked the question that turned the mundane table talk into a viable discussion.

"How much of Arizona *have* you seen?"

Karla finished chewing a tender piece of beef before replying with a sigh, "Very little, I'm afraid. I landed in Phoenix and drove to Sedona, but most of my attention was centered on the highway, so I noticed little of the passing scenery." She brightened. "But I did drive miles out of the way to enter Oak Creek Canyon via the scenic route from Flagstaff." As did her friends two days before, she recalled.

"And since you've been in Sedona?" he inquired, slicing a bite-size piece from his charbroiled steak.

Karla sipped at her drink. "Well, I toured the town fairly thoroughly while searching out a location for the gallery, but things got pretty frantic while I was getting the place ready for the opening, so I had precious little time to do much sight-seeing." He opened his mouth to comment, but she quickly added, "I did explore the courtyards with the surrounding galleries, shops, and restaurants in Tlaquepaque though."

Jared's fork paused midway between his mouth and his plate. "You haven't been to the Chapel of the Holy Cross?" Incredulity shaded his tone.

"Oh, yes." Karla laughed. "Anne, my assistant,

dragged me there the day after I hired her."

"And?"

"And I was impressed, of course," she admitted readily. "I mean, who wouldn't be impressed? It isn't every day that one comes across a clean-lined, austerely designed chapel set among jutting rocks at the very base of a towering cliff."

Jared chuckled in appreciation of her vivid description, and suddenly positive she could become addicted to the sound of his laughter, Karla finished off her margarita to quench her recently acquired raging thirst.

"Another?" Jared inclined his head to indicate the empty glass.

"Why not?" Karla replied on impulse.

"So your sight-seeing has been limited to the immediate area," he mused, raising his hand to summon the waiter.

"Umm," Karla concurred absently, giving her attention to scooping the last of the potato from the skin.

"Amazing."

Karla popped the forkful of potato into her mouth before raising puzzled eyes to his. "Pardon?" she mumbled.

Having captured the waiter's attention, Jared motioned for fresh drinks for both of them. He shrugged as he turned his attention to her. "I find it amazing that you are presuming to present and sell artworks depicting a region you have not visited," he explained.

Torn between laughter and astonishment, Karla just stared at him for several seconds. "I have never been to the moon, either," she said tauntingly when she finally found her voice. "Yet I wouldn't hesitate to present and sell an artist's conception of it."

"Good point," Jared conceded, then proceeded to demolish her argument. "But it has one flaw: Short of signing on for some future expedition to the moon, you have no choice but to accept an artist's concept of it." His smile returned her taunt in triplicate. "Whereas, in regard to modern western art, you are smack-dab in the middle of your subject. You do yourself and your customer a disfavor by your failure to initiate a personal exploration of it."

He was right. It galled Karla to admit it, even to herself, but he was right. Annoyed more by having Jared point out her professional oversight than by the oversight itself, Karla speared her fork into the last remaining sliver of meat. As she methodically chewed the beef, she concluded that, as much as she disliked having him criticize her, she would have to admit that he had a point.

"Okay. I give up. You win," she said with enforced good humor. "I will make it my personal mission to explore the modern West and all its art forms."

"When?"

The arrival of the waiter at the table with their drinks spared Karla the ignominy of completely losing her composure and shouting at Jared to mind his own business. She simmered while the man inquired if they would care for dessert, and shook her head sharply in the negative when Jared asked her if she'd like coffee. Jared's quirked eyebrow brought her to her senses.

"I'll go exploring when I have the time," she said reasonably, smiling at the waiter when he thanked them for their patronage.

Adding his own response, and a more than generous tip, Jared waited until the waiter walked away before saying flatly, "Take the time."

Karla was stunned and more than a trifle angered by

his directive. "Look," she said tightly. "There are less than two weeks until Thanksgiving, and in case you've forgotten, after Thanksgiving comes Christmas." She paused to gulp a quick swallow of her fresh drink. "I hope . . . plan, to do a brisk business during the weeks before Christmas. I can't afford to go sight-seeing at this time." Positive she'd made her position clear, she sat back and smiled at him.

Jared didn't return her smile; he pointed out the error in her reasoning. "On the contrary," he corrected. "During the busy weeks before Christmas you will need all the expertise you can acquire. Therefore, you can't afford *not* to go at this particular time."

Checkmate.

Karla wanted to scream. Or laugh. Or cry. Instead, she did some fast and serious thinking. If Jared's argument was valid, she could possibly double the holiday sales she was hoping for and, in consequence, not only establish herself firmly in the business community but pare away a large chunk out of her debts. Either result would be worth the time away from the gallery, but both . . .

Karla sat up abruptly. "Would it be possible to acquire this expertise, say, between now and Thanksgiving?" she asked thoughtfully. Only later did Karla realize that the satisfied curve to his smile really should have warned her.

"With a well-informed guide," he replied smoothly. "Yes, I think it would be possible."

Having missed the warning sign, Karla walked into the trap. "Can you recommend a well-informed guide?"

Jared's smile deepened. "Yes."

Karla didn't notice. "Is he very expensive?"

"Not at all."

She reached for her handbag to rummage through it for a pen and paper, and missed the crinkle of laugh lines at the corners of his eyes and mouth. "Will you give me his name and address?" she asked, pen poised to record the information.

"Certainly." Jared's voice was bone dry. "His name is Jared Cradowg and he lives at—" He paused when the pen dropped from her hand. "Is something wrong?" he asked innocently, smiling into her scowling face.

"Not something," she snapped. "Everything's wrong. Starting with you this morning, and ending with you right now." Convinced he was amusing himself at her expense, and inexplicably hurt because of it, Karla found herself fighting a desperate need to weep. "If you're quite finished," she continued in a suspiciously husky voice, "I'd like to go home now." Moving carefully, as if afraid she'd shatter with any undo haste, she began to slide her chair away from the table.

"Karla, I am dead serious."

The sincerity in Jared's low voice halted her action. Her hands gripping the chair, Karla gazed up at him. "About what?" she ridiculed. "Being my guide or becoming my lover?"

"Both," he admitted bluntly. "But I'll begin by introducing you to the splendor of the West and, I hope, end by introducing you to the delights of the flesh."

Karla gasped, then blushed, then laughed. "You don't pull your punches, do you?"

Jared laughed with her. "Never." He raised his eyebrows. "Well, what's it to be? Are you feeling adventurous—or are you going to give in to fear and run away and hide from me?"

In truth, Karla wanted to run for her life. But he had issued a challenge, thrown down the gauntlet, as it were. Studying his chiseled features, she weighed her decision with the same amount of care with which she weighed the value of every piece of work she accepted for display in her gallery. Yet, when she answered, Karla wasn't sure which of them was more surprised.

"You're on."

CHAPTER FOUR

SHE HAD TO be out of her tiny mind! Whatever had possessed her to accept Jared's challenge?

The back-to-back thoughts leaped into Karla's mind at the same instant she closed and locked her apartment door. Deep into contemplation, she absently hung her cape in the closet. A frown wrinkling her brow, she nibbled on her lip as she wandered into her bedroom.

What sort of game was Jared playing?

Karla slowly undressed as she examined the query. Considering his ardor in the gallery that morning, and again in her living room earlier that evening, in addition to his repeated assurances that they would be lovers, she had nervously anticipated a renewal of his efforts during the short drive back to her apartment after they left the restaurant. Yet, strangely, Jared's behavior had been scrupulously circumspect. Not only had he said very little, he hadn't so much as attempted to kiss her good night!

In retrospect, Karla was quickly coming to the conclusion that she had walked into a neatly laid trap. She knew intuitively that Jared hadn't abandoned his stated intention of having a love affair with her, but had simply altered his tactics.

Speculating on what his new tactics might be, Karla prepared for bed, automatically performing her nightly rituals of applying a facial mask, then soaking in a warm bath while the goop tightened on her face. The process should have been soothing; it usually worked, relaxing her for sleep . . . This night it failed.

Karla wasn't soothed. She wasn't relaxed. She was restless and edgy and wide awake. Her neatly made bed held no appeal; she skirted around it as she prowled the confines of her room. She let her thoughts dart in all directions, in a frantic attempt to avoid confronting the central issue—that being her own incredible response to Jared.

But eventually weariness and irrefutable fact caught up with her. Sighing in defeat, Karla shrugged out of her robe and crawled between the smooth, cool sheets. After settling in, she shut her eyes. She didn't want to think, didn't want to remember, didn't want to face her own physical and emotional betrayal. Seeking a means of escape, she wanted, longed for, the oblivion of sleep.

It was not to be. Five months of driving herself without mercy had marked her. She was hyper, wired, too tired to unwind naturally. At intervals, her mind drifted in a pleasant daze; then, with a start, she'd awaken, her heart thumping, her lips hot and dry, her breasts tingling, and her body aching with emptiness.

It had been so long, so very long a time since Karla

had known the fullness of a man . . . and even then it had not been a satisfying fullness. Memory stirred, and she winced.

Louis.

She moved her head restlessly on her pillow. Karla had banished the memory of Louis and the one-sided relationship they'd had. She didn't want to recall the time she'd spent with him, didn't want to remember how young and gullible she'd been. But Karla was tired, too tired to maintain her vigilance at the gates of remembrance. Groaning in protest, she shut her eyes. In flashing and painful color, the memories flooded her exhausted mind.

Karla had been eighteen and a freshman in college when she met Louis at an impromptu get-to-know-one-another party in the off-campus home of a classmate. Because of their mutual interest in art, her friend had introduced Karla to Louis, invited them to help themselves to the drinks and food, then had left them to fend for themselves.

Louis fended for himself very well.

Within three weeks of their first date, two days after the party, Louis had talked her into going to bed with him by the simple method of convincing her she was in love with him. The experience of physical initiation had not been an enjoyable one for Karla. Louis had confidently assured her that it would get better with practice, and as he was already a senior and three years older than she, Karla believed him. Yet, even with practice, *it* never did get better.

But, being young and believing she was in love, Karla eagerly tried to make up for—in Louis's opinion —her inability to give herself freely to the magnitude of the experience.

Though hesitant at first, she finally gave in to his plea to move into his studio flat. Then, although she knew they couldn't afford it, she gave in to his persuasive plea to move to a larger apartment. Soon she gave in to his next argument: Since he was in his senior year and therefore his studies were more important than hers, she should take fewer classes and work part-time to supplement their student loans. Before long, giving in to Louis's cleverly worded suggestions became a habit. And so, when he looked at her soulfully one afternoon and told her with a deep sigh that they needed still more money, Karla dropped out of school altogether to work full-time.

Dangling the carrot of his promise of future marriage in front of her, Louis kept her running for close to two years, straight through his graduation and into the first year of his postgraduate study. But he had miscalculated about one very important thing; Louis confidently believed he could keep Karla gullible for as long as it suited his purposes.

But though Karla was young, she was definitely not stupid. And though she no longer attended classes, she was receiving the equivalent of a doctorate in human nature as a full-fledged member of the working class. She earned an excellent salary that evaporated like smoke, blown away by the rent and the utilities and the paints and supplies and food that Louis consumed with the voracious appetite of a teenager.

As the second anniversary of their being together approached, and there was still no gold band on her left ring finger, Karla examined her life, her heart, and her soul and came to an enlightening, though painful conclusion.

Louis was not in love with her. She had been a convenience to his well-being and comfort. He had used her without compunction. Surprisingly, the realization didn't hurt as much as it should have. What inflicted the deepest hurt inside Karla was acknowledging the fact that, not only was she not in love with him, she had willingly allowed herself to be used. When she walked away from him, leaving behind everything she had worked so hard to provide for them, Karla carried a vow never to allow herself to be used by anyone, ever again.

The years that followed the breakup had not been easy. By working long hours, and limiting herself to only the bare necessities, Karla had paid off the debts she had accrued while living with Louis. Then she began saving, ferreting away the funds she needed to return to college for her degree. During her college years, she continued to work part-time. To save money, she had given up her precious privacy to share an apartment with two young women she met soon after arriving on campus. The three of them had been drawn together because they were of the same age and in the same financial circumstances. And although Karla despaired over many of the decisions she had made, she never regretted joining forces with Alycia and Andrea.

There had been moments, many in number, when loneliness caught her unaware and she had felt a gnawing need for something or someone. She got through those moments by sheer willpower and unremitting dedication to her goals: getting her degree and owning her own gallery. Despite the hard work involved, and the debts incurred, Karla was satisfied with her life.

And now another man wanted to use her for his own purposes.

That knowledge alone normally would not have bothered Karla; a variety of men over the years had wanted her for a variety of reasons. No, what kept her sleepless and restless was the acknowledgment of her own body's sudden clamoring demands for appeasement.

Karla didn't need the complication of a man in her life, and yet she had elected to accept Jared's challenge by agreeing to let him act as her guide and instructor on a sight-seeing jaunt around Arizona and parts west and unknown. And considering her quivering senses and aching body—never mind the hot, melting sensation she experienced at the mere sight of Jared Cradowg— she could see no way of getting through two weeks alone with him without succumbing to her own as well as his obvious desire.

At some subconscious level, had she deliberately agreed to go with Jared because she secretly wanted his "inevitable" affair to happen? The speculation sent molten heat searing through Karla, causing a tremor in her thighs and a tightness in her breasts.

Dammit, she wanted him! And why shouldn't she have him? She had known the lovemaking of one man only, and she was nearly twenty-seven years old! Why shouldn't she have him . . . if only for two short weeks?

The inner heat slowly cooled as she argued with herself, and rationality returned. The price of indulging herself with Jared could prove to be very high in the coin of emotional injury. Sitting up in the rumpled bed, Karla shook her head and muttered her earlier thought out loud, "No doubt about it, you are out of your tiny mind."

Startled by the ragged sound of her own voice, Karla laughed aloud and raised her hand to her mouth to muffle a sleepy yawn. Her eyes felt gritty, her eyelids heavy. Suddenly the tension drained from her, leaving her limp. With another wider yawn, she snuggled back under the covers.

She had resolved nothing by raking up the past or speculating on the future, but as she floated in a delicious warmth in the nether regions between wakefulness and sleep, Karla didn't care. She was comfortable. She was relaxed. She'd forget the past and let the future take care of itself.

With yet another yawn, Karla curled into her favorite sleep position. Her eyes drifted closed. A smile of contentment feathered her mouth. Then a nagging memory sprang into her mind: *his grandfather!*

Karla's eyes popped open and her lips curved into a frown as she tried to recall precisely what Jared had said about the disputed painting that had precipitated their first meeting. His exact phrasing eluded her—she was too sleepy to concentrate—but it had had something to do with the painting being a portrait of his grandfather. Now, what . . .?

Karla lost the battle; unconsciousness claimed her.

The next morning she overslept, and as Karla rarely overslept, she felt rushed and not quite organized. She didn't like the feeling and so, of course, she blamed Jared.

It was all his fault, she fumed, striding to the rear exit of the gallery after parking her car in back of the building. To her way of thinking, her rattled mental condition was a direct result of a progression of events, every one of which had been instigated by Jared Cradowg, beginning with his boorish behavior the night of the grand opening of the gallery, continuing with his deliberate assault on her senses, and ending with the clever trap he had rigged to ensnare her into agreeing to accompanying him on an educational sight-seeing trip with himself as guide.

Well, it was out of the question, Karla decided, rejecting her late-night weakness in the light of a new day. Unlocking the door, she stepped into the gallery office. She could not—no, would not!—go with him. As if to punctuate and enforce her decision, she slammed the door.

"Are you sure it's shut?"

Karla started, both at the unexpected sound of the male voice and at the dry amusement in it. Suddenly breathless, and annoyed because of it, she glared at the tall man propped lazily in the doorway to the showroom.

"Have you decided to make a career of frightening me every morning?" she demanded, but continued before he could respond, "What are you doing here?"

Jared's soft laughter did a skip-jump down her spine. "Is this a quiz?" he asked in a teasing drawl. Then, following her example, he went on without waiting for a reply. "Will there be a prize for the correct answer?"

Karla gritted her teeth and made a strangled sound deep in her throat.

"Is that a yes or a no?" he prompted.

"You . . . you . . ." Karla drew a sharp breath. "What do you want at this hour of the morning?" she cried in a voice drawn tight by the resurgence of nocturnal memories.

Jared shook his head sadly. "No prize for that answer," he murmured, as if to himself. "The question's much too easy."

A sensation of feeling harried yet excited was too much for Karla's patience to bear. Her control snapped, and so did she. "Get on with it!"

"Yes, ma'am." Jared's indolent attitude vanished as he straightened and moved toward her with long purposeful strides. "A prize indeed," he said with satisfaction, pulling her into his arms. "And I didn't even answer the questions." Ignoring her startled gasp, he lowered his head and crushed her mouth beneath his.

His kiss was at once possessive and demanding . . . of everything—her submission, her participation, her passion. Karla longed for the strength to deny his demand, but it would have been like denying herself the necessity to breathe. The piercing thrust of his searching tongue rent the invisible fabric of tension cloaking her. Karla's body softened to meld with the masculine hardness of his. Their tongues engaged in a sweetly erotic duel that sent rapier thrusts of heat to every pleasure point in her body. She shuddered and moaned when his hand skimmed with tantalizing slowness up her rib cage to capture one already taut, aching breast.

"Does that answer your question?" Jared asked against her moist, trembling lips. "I want you." His lips blazed a fiery trail down her arched throat. "I want you in the morning. I want you at night." His tongue probed the shallow hollow at the base of her throat; his voice held a note of near desperation. "I wanted you all last night."

Since it reminded her of her own uncomfortable night, Jared's confession effectively destroyed the resolution Karla had made moments before. "I know," she whispered, moaning as his fingers found and explored the hardening tip of her breast.

"Do you?" Jared raised his head to stare into her passion-cloudy eyes. "Yes, you do know," he answered for her. "You want me now, this instant, don't you, sweetheart?"

Karla should have resented the blatant manner in which he was taking advantage of the situation and her, and somewhere deep inside she did. She was just too sense-oriented at that moment to dredge the resentment to the surface. The best she could manage was to refuse him a vocal response.

"Karla?" Jared's soft voice held a promise of paradise.

Hanging on to that promise somewhere deep inside, Karla shook her head obstinately.

"I can make you answer, you know," he said with obvious enjoyment, wringing a gasp from her with his long, dexterous fingers.

Unable to speak because of the anticipatory thrill zigzagging through her, Karla again shook her head. Her breath tangled in her throat at the slow smile that twitched the corners of his mouth an instant before he dipped his head and pressed his smiling lips to the shimmering silky material clinging to her breast.

As a form of punishment, the sensuous movement of his lips was exquisite torture. Karla's thinking process dissolved; there was no gallery, no work to be done, no patrons to be catered to. Time hung suspended; there was no day or night. All that was, all that existed, was the excruciating pleasure of Jared's mouth and hands and body pressed to hers. Reality was an intrusion that activated and enraged the deeply buried resentment; reality intruded in the voice of her assistant.

"Karla, I— Oh! Oh, Lord!"

Jared did not rear back in guilty haste. Keeping one arm firmly around Karla's waist, he straightened and eased around to gaze somberly at Anne.

"I . . . I am sorry." The color in Anne's cheeks rivaled the splash of red in a western sunset. "I . . . ah . . . had no

idea..." She ground to a helpless halt, her glance dart-
ing from her employer to the tall man standing in a
protective arch over her.

In contrast to the blush tingeing Anne's cheeks, acute
embarrassment washed every trace of color from Karla's
face. She opened her mouth to speak, but Jared was
obviously thinking much faster.

"No apology necessary," he assured the stricken
young woman. "If you will give us a moment," he suggested, "I will remove myself from the premises."

"Oh!" The color fluctuated wildly beneath Anne's
smooth young skin. "Yes, of course!" Spinning around,
she fled from the office into the showroom.

Jared's soft laughter released the lock of mortifica-
tion on Karla's throat. "Oh, Lord!" She groaned. "I
can't imagine what Anne must be thinking."

"I can."

The dry amusement in his voice drew Karla's dazed
eyes to his face. His nearly black eyes held an obsidian
gleam, the squint lines at the corners of his eyes were
deeply creased, his lips twitched suspiciously, and the
muscles along his jawline quivered from his clenching
restraint. Shaking free of his supporting arm, she
backed two distancing steps away from him. "You think
it's funny?" she demanded indignantly.

Jared's control broke and his laughter erupted, flood-
ing Karla's senses with the sound of his amusement.
"Damn straight, it's funny." He flicked his hand to indicate the doorway through which Anne had escaped.

"Sure, you can laugh!" Karla fumed. "But I have to
go in there and face 'that pretty little thing.'" She drew
a harsh breath, then exhaled a long sigh. "What in the
world am I going to say to her?"

His shrug was both careless and elegant. The sinewy

movement of his broad shoulders mesmerized Karla for a moment. Jared's dryly delivered advice quickly brought her back to the reality of her uncomfortable situation. "You don't have to say anything." He gave her a chiding smile.

"Oh, how very profound!" she grumbled, frowning as she attempted to tuck a dislodged lock of her hair into the businesslike coil at the nape of her neck.

"I wasn't trying to be profound." His tone held an impatient yet vague note. "You don't really need to explain anything to Anne or anyone else. You're the boss."

The distracted sound of his voice snagged her attention. Glancing at him, Karla felt the breath catch in her chest at the dark intensity of his stare. "What—" she began to ask, but, as if he didn't hear her, Jared spoke over her voice in a rough-edged murmur.

"Is it very long?"

Karla blinked. "What?"

Jared shifted his brooding gaze to hers. "Your hair," he explained. "It's such a rich, lustrous shade of brown. Is it very long?"

Karla swallowed to wet her suddenly parched throat. "Shoulder-length," she answered in a dry crackle.

"I want to touch it, tangle my fingers in it."

From the corner of her eye, Karla saw his fingers flex. Her scalp began to tingle, and she felt herself melt inside. As if drawn by the magnet of his dark eyes, her body swayed toward him.

"Yes," Jared breathed encouragingly.

No! Karla caught herself up short. Squaring her shoulders, she raised her arm and pointed to the exit door. "Out!" she ordered in a tight voice.

Jared's smile told her he was fully aware of the conflict raging inside of her. "Not until we've settled our business." He shook his head, and a lock of his rough-cut, unruly hair ruffled then came to rest on his forehead.

Karla's fingers itched with a desire to smooth the gleaming black strands into place. Denying the urge, she lowered her arm and clasped her hands behind her back. "What business?" she asked, narrowing her eyes with suspicion.

"You know very well what business." He arched one eyebrow mockingly. "Or have you conveniently forgotten the sight-seeing trip we discussed last night?"

Surprisingly—or maybe not so surprisingly, considering the mush his ardor had made of her mind—Karla *had* forgotten about the trip. Along with his reminder came the jolting remembrance of the decision she'd made a scant fifteen minutes earlier to cancel out of the arrangement. "Ah . . . Jared—"

"Ah, Jared, nothing," he cut her off ruthlessly. "I have no intention of allowing you to back out of it."

Karla bristled. "You have no intention!" she exclaimed. "And exactly how do you think you could stop me from backing out of it?"

He smiled, very slowly, and took a step toward her. "Shall we treat your assistant to a repeat performance of how strong-willed you are?" he asked in a silky tone.

Absolutely refusing to retreat before his advance, Karla clenched her jaw and held her ground. "I'm warning you, Jared. Don't touch me." Karla despaired at the lack of conviction in her wavering voice.

Jared looked intrigued. "Or—what?"

Outflanked, and too aware of her precarious position, Karla closed her eyes. "Jared, don't." She opened her eyes to stare at him with unconcealed entreaty. "I have work to do." To her disbelief, his eyes softened.

"Have dinner with me tonight at my place."

His voice held a plea that expanded her disbelief to sheer amazement. Not trusting the sound of it, or him, Karla eyed him warily. "I don't think so."

"Don't think about it," he said with hard emphasis. "*Feel* about it."

Since it was the *feeling* she feared, Karla slowly shook her head.

"Karla . . . please."

The coaxing allure of his low, crooning voice proved stronger than Karla's power of resistance. Her emotions in conflict, she stared at him, absorbing the look, the essence of him into her senses.

Even as a supplicant, Jared was formidable. Though his eyes were soft, they stared at her from a chiseled face taut with inner tension. His back was ramrod straight. His broad shoulders and chest were tight with ridged muscles. His arms hung loose at his sides, but his fingers were curled into hard fists. His long legs were separated to balance his torso, the rigidly straight, inverted V tapering from muscular calves to hard thighs to narrow hips and flat belly. The civilizing camouflage of fashionable clothing enhanced the exciting uncivilized look of him.

Karla stared, and absorbed, and conceded defeat. "What time?"

Jared moved. She started.

"Don't panic." His laughter increased the flow of color to her cheeks.

"You make me edgy," Karla admitted without thinking.

Jared's laughter ceased abruptly. "I know," he said seriously. "The reaction is mutual."

Karla's eyes widened in surprise, but before she could assemble a reply, he was moving... toward the door. He grasped the shiny metal knob as if fighting a need to tear it from its moorings. "What time?" he repeated in a low growl.

Karla wasn't the least bit frightened by his tone or the harsh set of his features. She was trembling, but she wasn't frightened. Her tremors were a surface reaction to the fire of excitement zipping through her.

"Seven?" she asked in a husky whisper.

"Six-thirty," he said flatly.

She held out an instant, fighting his attraction and her own needs. Then she sighed and surrendered. "I'll be ready."

The effect on Jared was immediate and startling. He went stone still; then a shudder rippled the length of his tall frame. His fingers opened, releasing the doorknob, then closed again in a crushing grip.

Attuned to him, Karla was aware of his emotions on every level of her being. For seconds that stretched out toward the boundaries of eternity they stared into each other's eyes. The feet and inches separating them remained the same, yet there was no distance. They were as one. She felt his passions; he knew her fears.

Then, abruptly, Jared twisted the knob and pulled the door open, and the boundaries of infinity receded.

Karla blinked herself back into reality.

"Six-thirty," he reiterated.

Her gaze fastened to his, Karla nodded. Memory stirred as he turned to leave; as he stepped outside, she blurted, "Jared, wait! There's something I want to know!"

Turning his head, Jared looked at her over his

shoulder, one eyebrow inching up in question. "And that is?"

Karla motioned at the door to the gallery. "The painting," she explained in a rush. "Last night, you mentioned something about your grandfather. Did you mean the painting is actually a—"

"A portrait of my grandfather?" Jared finished for her.

"Yes."

Jared's smile outsparkled the brilliant morning sunlight. "Yes."

"But . . ."

"Tonight, sweetheart." With the soft promise, Jared was gone, leaving Karla frowning in consternation at the closed door.

CHAPTER FIVE

"YOU'VE BEEN STARING at that canvas for almost an hour." The edgy sound of Anne's voice broke into Karla's deep thoughts. "I'm beginning to think the painting has enchanted you."

Tearing her bemused stare from the portrait of Jared's grandfather, Karla turned to smile absently at her frowning assistant.

"Or is it the painter who has enchanted you?" Anne didn't return Karla's smile. In fact, her lips compressed into a tight line.

The undercurrent of disapproval in Anne's tone confused Karla. Her smile faded as she studied her assistant. Anne's small, slender form was stiff; her features were pinched. Her attitude was puzzling, especially coming after the hero-worship the younger woman had displayed on the opening night of the gallery. It didn't make sense. Unless...

Karla's gaze sharpened on the expression of censure on her assistant's face as she recalled the passionate scene Anne had witnessed earlier in the office. Could it be possible that the girl was jealous?

Compassion stirred in Karla. Her smile was soft, her voice gentle. "What's bothering you, Anne?"

"Him!" In an almost violent gesture, Anne flung her hand out to indicate the painting.

Impatience strained the bounds of her compassion at the disparaging harshness of Anne's voice. Karla's smile vanished. Conflicting feelings rushed through her —revival of the embarrassment she'd suffered at having been observed in a compromising position with Jared, and anger at Anne's contemptuous reference to him. Deciding the air between them needed to be cleared at once, she drew a deep breath and tried to maintain her composure.

"And what is it about *him* that bothers you?" Karla's voice was clipped, her words measured.

"He can hurt you, Karla!" Anne cried, impulsively reaching out to grasp her hand. "And I'd hate to see that happen to you! You're too good for that."

Now Karla was thoroughly confused. Anne's anguished tone conveyed genuine concern, which eliminated the possibility of jealousy. Karla shook her head. "Too good for what? Anne, what would you hate to see happen to me?"

"Jared Cradowg." Anne said his name as if the very sound of it was distasteful.

Karla was stunned. "Anne, I don't understand," she said, when she could finally speak. "The other night you were thrilled by the very sight of him. And now. . ." She lifted her shoulders in a helpless shrug.

Anne's grasp tightened urgently on Karla's hand. "I was thrilled by the presence of the artist, not the man," she explained.

Karla frowned. "But the artist *is* the man, Anne!" she exclaimed.

"No!" Anne said in sharp denial. "The artist is touched by genius. The man is tainted by ruthlessness."

"Oh, Anne, really." Karla sighed in exasperation. Though it was true she had swiftly concluded that Jared possessed more than his share of arrogance and over-confidence, in her opinion, Anne's expression, "tainted by ruthlessness," was more than a bit too much. "Aren't you being a little melodramatic?" she asked gently.

Anne shook her head vigorously. "If anything, I'm not stating it strongly enough!" When Karla met her declaration with a dry look, Anne's eyes grew wide with disbelief. "Haven't you heard the gossip and rumors about him?"

Karla's chin snapped up. "I never listen to gossip or rumors, Anne! The information is generally unfair, not to mention distorted."

Anne smiled and sighed. "I agree with you in principle," she avowed, "but in this instance, I really think you should have listened."

"Why?" Karla asked, vaguely uneasy.

"Because most of it is true." Anne's smile was cynical. "The genius himself has admitted it."

Karla didn't want to know. She didn't want to hear whatever it was Anne was so obviously anxious to tell her. Her lips were still tingling from the heat of Jared's mouth; her senses were still in a heightened state of awareness. Every inch of her body continued to ache for every inch of his.

Dammit! Karla protested silently, curling her fingers into her palms. She didn't want to know!

She was on the point of dismissing the subject by turning away from Anne when a vivid memory flashed into her mind. Too sharply, Karla recalled Jared's behavior and his insulting remarks to her two nights before.

Was Jared capable of ruthlessness? she asked herself. The answer came into her mind at once. Yes, she believed he could be ruthless if he chose to be. Karla's shoulders drooped in resignation.

"All right, Anne," she said wearily. "Suppose you fill in the blanks for me."

Anne bit her lip. "Karla, please understand that I mentioned it only because I don't want you to get hurt."

Karla nodded, convinced by the younger woman's dismay that she was not acting out of jealousy or the viciousness that motivated most gossips. "I understand," she murmured, "and I appreciate your concern."

"Well, for one thing—" Anne began, but broke off, glancing at the door when a customer entered the gallery. "Shall I take care of him?" she asked, indicating the elderly gentleman, who smiled rather timidly at them.

"No, I'll do it," Karla replied, returning the man's smile. "But you could make a pot of coffee. It's almost lunchtime, and we haven't even had our morning break."

Karla spent close to half an hour chatting with the affable gentleman, who was new to the world of art but eager to learn about it. Consequently, when she was free to join Anne in the back office, much of her inner tension had eased, due in no small degree to the profitable sale she had made to the man.

After seeing the customer out, Karla turned the discreet sign in the window so as to change the message from Open to Will Return in One Hour, then locked the door and, humming softly, walked to the office. The tension began to coil through her again at the sight that met her eyes as she entered the small room: Anne was seated at the desk, her narrow shoulders hunched, a brooding expression on her face, staring into a cup of coffee as if hoping to discover the answers to all her problems within the depths of the cream-laced liquid.

Suppressing a sigh, Karla squared her shoulders and walked briskly to the coffee maker, perched atop a metal file cabinet. "Okay, Anne, we have one hour," she said, filling a ceramic mug with the steaming brew before turning, eyebrows arched, to look at the young woman. "I suggest we get on with it."

The brown eyes Anne raised had a sad puppylike appeal. "You *are* somewhat enchanted by him, aren't you?"

Karla shrugged. The threat of losing an exorbitant sale wouldn't have forced her to confess to the confusing riot of sensations Jared had unleashed in her, enchantment being only one of them. "That's neither here nor there," she replied, lying through her teeth. "I'm a big girl, and quite capable of taking care of myself," she continued, feigning a confidence she was far from feeling. "Just give me the information you feel I must have, and I'll decide how to proceed from there."

"All right, you're the boss." Anne exhaled a long, soulful sigh. Then she frowned. "You do know that Jared's father, Rhys Cradowg, is a very important man in Arizona, don't you?"

Karla narrowed her eyes in thought as she rummaged through her memory file. She did remember the name, simply because it was so unusual, but was unable to come up with any solid information connected to it, and she said as much to Anne. "The name is familiar but . . ." She gave her assistant a deprecatory smile. "I'm afraid I was too involved with the hundred and one details necessary to launching the gallery to register any outside information." Her frown reflected Anne's. "Why? Is it imperative that I know how important Jared's father is?"

"Yes," Anne responded adamantly. "You see, Rhys Cradowg is, today, a broken man." She paused to sip her coffee—and, Karla decided later, for effect. "And he was broken by the single person capable of piercing his defenses . . . his son."

Though Karla experienced a resurgence of unease, she didn't feel at all enlightened. Frown lines deepening on her brow, she lowered herself onto the chair in front of the desk. "You've lost me already, Anne." Tired patience shaded Karla's tone. "Why would Jared want to harm his father?"

"Because of his Apache heritage."

"I don't believe I'm hearing this from you!" Karla exclaimed, jolting upright in her chair so abruptly that her coffee sloshed over the rim of the mug and splashed onto her hand. Jumping up, she set the mug on the desk with an angry-sounding bang. And Karla was angry, furiously angry. She deplored the sort of prejudice that Anne's statement hinted at—in effect, that because Jared was part Indian he was therefore part savage. Plucking a tissue from the box on the desk, she dabbed at the moisture on her hand while continuing to scowl at Anne. "Are you actually telling me that you believe Jared Cradowg is ruthless because he has Apache blood?"

Anne shook her head vigorously. "No, of course not!"

"Then what the hell are you saying?" Karla demanded, her anger still strong but tempered by the relief she felt. "Anne, I think you'd better start at the beginning."

Anne was trembling from the shock of being the target of Karla's unusual blast of fury. "I don't know all of it," she said in a tremulous whisper. "Only bits and pieces."

Karla's eyes widened. "Yet from these bits and pieces you pass judgment on a man's character?" The anger in her voice had given way to sheer astonishment.

"No!" Anne's expression clearly revealed her regret at having initiated the subject. "Oh, God! Karla, please, let me try to explain."

"I'd appreciate it," Karla replied wryly. Picking up her mug, she walked to the coffee maker. "Would you like a refill?" she asked over her shoulder in as natural a tone of voice as she could muster.

"Yes, thank you." Anne's whisper contained a wealth of gratitude for Karla's apparent attempt to restore a measure of normalcy. "I'm almost sorry I said anything," she murmured, as Karla handed a cup to her.

"'Almost' doesn't count," Karla said chidingly, returning to her chair. "Except in quoits," she tacked on dryly, offering the younger woman a wry smile.

With Anne's response to the smile, the tension eased. "I feel like a fool, or a snitch, or worse," she said, "but here goes." She drew a deep breath, then began speaking rapidly. "As I understand it, Jared always adored his grandfather, and deeply resented hearing his idol referred to as a half-breed. And since—"

"Wait!" Karla cried, holding up her hand. "Half-breed? Are you telling me that man in the portrait is not a full-blooded Apache?"

"Yes," Anne said flatly. "His mother was pure Apache, but his father was pure Welsh."

"Incredible," Karla breathed. "But that would explain Jared's unusual height."

"Well, I suppose," Anne said. "But I have heard of other, equally tall Indians. And, in Jared's case, his father, Rhys, is also both Welsh and very tall."

"I see," Karla murmured, comprehending how the traits of height and chiseled features and dark good looks, traits not unusual in both races, had manifested themselves in the compelling attractiveness of the man who made her senses reel and her blood run hot. "Continue," she said, suppressing a shivering response to her thoughts.

"As I said," Anne went on. "Jared resented the term 'half-breed,' which made life at home for him unpleasant while he was growing up, since it was apparently the only expression Rhys ever used in reference to his father-in-law."

"What?" Karla exclaimed. "But where was Jared's mother?"

"Right there." Anne sighed. "My understanding is that Rhys was very domineering, the absolute master of all he surveyed, from his vast ranch lands down to the smallest items he possessed, and his behavior even extended to his son and his wife—at least until her death about five years ago. I was told that Jared and Rhys had a terrible argument after she died and that, leaving everything but his painting supplies and the clothes on his back, Jared left his father's house for good less than half an hour after he had helped to lower his mother into the ground."

This time, Karla was unsuccessful at repressing a responsive shiver. "So Jared was raised on a ranch," she mused aloud, unsurprised, since everything about him, from his long-muscled ranginess to his sun-darkened skin and his earthy appeal spoke of a man who had grown up close to the land.

"One of the largest ranches in the entire Southwest," Anne said emphatically. "And those in a position to know claim that Jared is an even more expert cattleman than his father ever was."

"And he has never gone back?" Karla asked, unable to believe that anyone could sever such strong bonds that easily.

Anne shook her head. "Not as far as anyone knows. But I've heard that Jared and Rhys have locked horns several times since then, and that Rhys has come out the loser every time."

Karla was quiet a moment, digesting the story. Then she frowned at Anne. "I'm not sure I quite understand why you or anyone else would call Jared ruthless because of his actions. I mean, everyone knew how much Jared loved his grandfather, and they knew that Rhys mistreated the older man," she added, keeping Anne silent with a flick of her hand. "I would think that people would call Rhys ruthless and offer Jared sympathy and compassion."

"But that's just it!" Anne exclaimed. "Jared did receive sympathy and compassion—at least when he first took up residence here in Sedona. But he turned the sentiment against himself by his coldness and his arrogant attitude."

"But surely his attitude was understandable, under the circumstances!" Karla protested, telling herself she was defending her outraged sense of fair play, and not the man under discussion. But she knew, deep inside, that she was lying to herself; she was strongly defending the man.

"Up to a point, yes!" Anne argued. "But only up to a point. And that point was reached and exceeded not once but many times." She paused for a sip of the now tepid coffee before explaining. "The first point occurred when his father had a massive stroke after one of their confrontations—apparently an unusually vicious one. Rhys was very close to death and calling for . . . begging for Jared—and that has been confirmed by his doctors." She drew a sharp breath, as if angered by the memory. "Jared refused to see him, both in private, to his father's doctors, and later very publicly."

"Publicly?" Karla repeated. She suddenly felt exhausted, and the tension and uneasiness had returned to claw at her nervous system.

"Yes." Anne's voice reflected Karla's weariness. "In all fairness I must say that Jared didn't seek publicity. Quite the contrary, he shunned it assiduously. But as it happened, an overeager television newsman from Phoenix decided to follow Jared for a few nights, in the hope of sniffing out a juicy segment to spice up the late news. The second night he got lucky. He followed Jared to Flagstaff, to the home of his then current lady love." Anne lowered her gaze at Karla's involuntary shudder at the term "lady love," but continued doggedly. "There was a camera crew waiting when Jared emerged from the house, looking tired and irritable, early the next morning. I saw the newscast that evening, and I must admit the reporter badgered Jared. But that was no excuse for what he finally said when the man persisted in questioning him about Rhys."

Of course, Karla had to ask. "What did he say?"

"He said, 'Let him die and go to hell, because that's exactly where he belongs.'"

Not even attempting to conceal the appalling shock she was feeling, Karla closed her eyes. How could Jared say anything so unspeakably cruel about his own father, regardless of the provocation? It was beyond her comprehension how anyone could wish for the death of *any* person, let alone his own flesh and blood. For long minutes an unnatural quiet gripped her and the small room. Anne's raggedly in-drawn breath shattered the silence.

"That's only part of it, Karla."

Karla gazed at Anne with dulled eyes. "You might as well finish." Her voice was as dull as her eyes. "I don't see how it could get much worse."

Anne's expression should have warned Karla how wrong she was. The young woman winced and bit her lip. "It concerns his . . . ah, women."

"Women?" Karla sat up straight, the dullness in her eyes and tone replaced by sharp alertness. "How many women?"

Anne shrank back in the leather desk chair. "I don't know the exact number. There are only four that I am certain of."

"Only four!" There wasn't a hint of humor in Karla's abortive burst of laughter. "Only four! Good Lord!"

"Yeah." Anne nodded her head solemnly. "That's the way most people feel."

Distracted by the sickening memory of her thrilled and flattered response to the person who was emerging as the modern man's answer to a modern Casanova, Karla hadn't absorbed Anne's remark. "What?" she asked blankly.

"I said that most people share your shock," Anne

explained. "From all indications, Jared is as ruthless with women as he is with his own father." Her soft eyes grew dark with concern. "He apparently takes on and discards women with less care than he gives to his clothes. He's a user, Karla. And that's why I was so upset. I think you're too good for that, too good for him."

Another user.

The thought, and all the painful memories it conjured, nagged at Karla's mind throughout the afternoon, but she hid her distress well.

Karla's defense mechanism kicked into gear moments after Anne finished speaking her impassioned thoughts. Inside, Karla was a seething mass of conflicting emotions, impressions, and reactions. Outwardly, she had turned to ice. She allowed none of her feelings to show—none.

The day dragged on . . . too quickly.

Karla's nerves tightened by increments with every glance she sent to the narrow watch encircling her wrist. She had agreed to have dinner with Jared at his place. He would be coming for her, no doubt with seduction in mind, at six-thirty.

Karla had a decision to make. And she was too quickly running out of time.

Customers came, customers went, and several left a tidy sum of money for purchases made. Karla appeared relaxed, talking and even laughing with the art patrons while discussing some of the finer points of various western art forms. Yet all the while, she scrupulously avoided glancing at the commanding canvas in the center of the display wall. With the possible exception of Anne, no one seemed to notice. And, having stated her opinion, Anne offered no further comment . . . that is, until they were locking up the gallery for the night.

"I'm sorry."

Though she felt herself grow stiff, Karla finished locking the back door before turning to stare at Anne. "There's no reason for you to feel sorry." Her smile was faint. "There was no malicious intent."

Anne's eyes flew wide open. "No! Of course not. But I've upset you"—she broke off to shake her head—"and after you've been so patient with me, explaining the business to me, being my friend." Again Anne hesitated, swallowing roughly. "Karla, I wanted to prevent you from being hurt . . . not hurt you myself!" she cried in a voice heavy with self-condemnation.

"I know." Karla smiled with understanding and compassion. "It's almost funny," she observed sadly. "Your life can be going along nicely, if hectically, and all it takes is the presence of one male to completely screw up the works." She exhaled harshly. "It has got to be the story of almost every female's life."

"Men hardly ever play fair."

Anne's assessment of the male of the species drew a small burst of genuine amusement from Karla. "Unfairness is an innate character flaw in all men; they don't know any better." She sighed. "I hope some future generation of truly liberated women will finally succeed in cleaning up *their* act."

Anne reluctantly gave in to a grin. "I'd love to be there to see it."

"Oh, so would I, more than you can imagine," Karla murmured in agreement. Her eyes narrowed as an image of another user flashed into her mind. Then she winced as Jared's strong visage swiftly superimposed itself on that of the other man. "But I can't envision that happening anytime soon, so I doubt we'll be around to witness the occasion." A bitter smile robbed her mouth of its natural softness. "The beasts are slow to learn."

Their slow pace revealing the weariness both were feeling, they walked to where their cars were parked side by side on the small macadam lot. As they separated, Anne moved her shoulders in a shrug of acceptance. "Well, as the saying goes, you can't live with 'em and you can't live without 'em."

As she slid behind the wheel of her car, Karla shot Anne a pained look. "Trite, very trite," she drawled. "But unfortunately also very true."

The extent of that truth slammed into Karla a short while later. During the drive home, her mind was by necessity occupied with the business of negotiating the after-work traffic. She simply didn't have time to ponder the information Anne had imparted to her. But it came rushing to overwhelm her the minute she shut her apartment door.

What was she going to do? Worrying the question, Karla slumped into a chair and stared into space. She had to make a decision, and she had to do it PDQ!

Reminded of the time, she glanced at her watch and felt the first stirrings of what she feared could grow into full-blown panic. Jared would be at her door in less than an hour!

She had to make a decision!

Bolting from her chair, Karla prowled around the tastefully decorated room, looking at everything, seeing nothing, until her restless glance collided with the elegant phone on the desk in one corner.

Find his number and call him, she ordered herself urgently. Tell him thanks, but no thanks—for his invitation to dinner, and his services as a guide, and most emphatically for his blatant insistence on the inevitability of an affair between them in the very near future.

Acting on the impulse, Karla strode purposefully to the desk. With every intention of calling Jared to advise him to turn his considerable charm to the seduction of some other, more gullible female, she reached for the phone. Her hand paused an inch from the receiver, arrested by the breath-reducing Technicolor image of him that filled her mind and weakened her knees—as well as her determination.

Fighting the thrill of remembered sensations, Karla could hear his beguiling voice, murmuring dark, exciting words of enticement. Her lips burned, her body ached, her senses urged her to recall the taste of him, the feel of him, and to forget everything she had heard that day.

Damn Jared Cradowg! she thought. And damn this attraction that drew her to him!

The silent cry shuddered through Karla's body. The inner battle was lost. Her hand fell away from the receiver, and as it fell Karla glanced at her watch. Jared would be arriving in less than half an hour!

At that moment, Karla wanted nothing so much as to run fast and far. Pride and simple economics kept her rooted to the floor. She had run away from one man; she'd be damned if she'd repeat the experience. Her pride would not allow retreat. Economically, she was bound to the gallery, and unless she physically removed herself from the scene, there was no possible way she could avoid contact with Jared. He was an artist, and not just any artist but a rather famous one at that. Karla knew that running was an option she couldn't afford.

She was back to square one, worrying the question and biting her lip as she raked her mind for an answer.

She was prodded into action by another glance at her watch. Spinning away from the desk, she strode from the living room to her bedroom. She made her decision midway between rooms. She would have dinner with him—nothing more.

Karla conceived a plan of procedure while standing under a senses-cooling shower, and committed herself to it while dressing and applying a light makeup with practiced swiftness.

She was vulnerable to Jared, more so than to any other man she had ever met, including the only man she had ever been intimate with. That vulnerability had to be protected.

Not being able to run from Jared did not mean that Karla could not hide. After years of withdrawing deep within herself, she was expert at hiding—her feelings, her emotions, her frustrations. Activating her defense mechanism, she attired her body in a soft, clingy apricot wool dress and cloaked her vulnerability in the armor of steely composure.

Recalling Jared's stated desire to see her hair unbound, Karla deftly coiled the long dark mass into a sleek twist at the nape of her neck. She was anchoring the last hairpin when the doorbell rang. She froze for an instant, nerves twanging. Then, raising her chin, she consciously brought her emotions under control by delivering a silent lecture.

She was not some quivering Victorian miss, subject to the whims of the superior male. She was an intelligent, well-educated woman of the twentieth century, independent and as "today" as the morning television news.

The doorbell rang again, a short, impatient summons that seemed to echo the whims of the superior male. At the imperious sound, Karla's lips formed a small, cool smile. Deciding that with the powerful incentive she now had, she should have no difficulty at all maintaining her composure, Karla scooped up her purse, left the bedroom, and calmly walked to the door and swung it open.

The sight of him tested Karla's resolve. Jared looked lean and sexy in brushed denims, a cable-knit pullover, and a suede jacket. Fortunately, he reinforced her determination with the first words out of his mouth: "I wanted you to let your hair down."

"Did you?" Karla arched her eyebrows and gave him a wry look. "I prefer it up."

His gaze sharpened as he examined her expression. "Are you angry about something?"

"Angry? No, I'm not angry." Try "wary," she thought, turning to retrieve her cape from the chair on which she'd tossed it on entering the apartment.

"Something's wrong," he insisted, moving to take the garment from her and hold it for her. "Was there a problem at the gallery today?"

Besides you?

Keeping the retort to herself, Karla shook her head. "No, no problem at the gallery," she answered ambiguously. "Actually, it was a very good day, for sales."

Though Jared frowned, he didn't question the slight emphasis she'd placed on the crucial word "sales." Anxious not to give him the opportunity to read between the lines, or to become amorous, Karla offered him a prodding smile. "I'm ready."

Jared relaxed and smiled back at her, too slowly, too sexily. "What for?" he asked softly.

Karla sent a silent command to cease and desist to pulses fluttering on the brink of rampant excitement.

"Dinner," she said succinctly. "I'm famished." To her complete surprise, she realized she was telling the truth. But then, she hadn't eaten since early that morning, and it had been a long, trying day, what with one thing and another.

He grinned and indicated the door with a flourish. "After you. I hope you like hot things."

Karla stiffened and stared at him warily. "Like what?"

"Like Mexican food." His grin grew positively wicked. "And me."

Determined not to allow him to rattle her, Karla maintained her cool. "I love Mexican food," she said. But as she swept past him she added, "I'm reserving judgment on you."

CHAPTER SIX

"YOU'VE CHANGED YOUR mind, haven't you?"

Karla shivered. The chill feathering her arms, raising goose bumps, had nothing to do with the outside temperature, or the fact that she was standing mere inches from the window that took up most of one wall in the living room of Jared's fantastic house. And fantastic was the only way to describe the house, which appeared to teeter on the very edge of a bluff. Of course, it was too dark for Karla to see what lay beneath the cliff, but Jared had told her the house overlooked Oak Creek and the valley beyond.

Karla could see the inside of the house, though, and immediately liked what she saw. The house was open, airy, thoroughly southwestern in design. The walls were smooth, stark white plaster. The exposed ceiling beams were stained a dark walnut. The furniture was casual,

comfortable, covered in natural fabrics with bright
splashes of earth tones—greens and browns and the oc-
casional dash of pumpkin.

In an odd, inexplicable way, Karla had felt at ease
and at home from the minute she'd crossed the threshold. Afraid to question the feeling, she had pushed it to
the back of her mind and let her senses absorb the ambience.

Surprisingly, although she had anticipated nervous-
ness, Karla had relaxed and enjoyed both the atmo-
sphere and Jared's interesting, if slightly strained,
conversation. And at his suggestion after they'd finished
dinner that they leave the cleaning up till later, Karla
had cradled her delicate wineglass in her hands and
strolled to the window, drawn by the darkness beyond.
She had been staring into that darkness for some minutes, raking her mind for yet another safe topic of discussion. The abruptness of his question banished her
sense of ease, creating tension not only in Karla but in
the spacious room that suddenly seemed too small to
contain the two of them.

She hadn't heard Jared come up behind her. She
hadn't seen him, either. Focusing on the wide window,
she took note of his reflection; it was so clear she could
even read his expression.

Jared was confused, impatient, and beginning to get
a little angry.

She had given him reason for the emotions. After her
unbridled response to him that morning, Karla could
well imagine his expectations for this evening. She had
thrown him a curve by acting aloof from the moment
she'd opened her door to him, and now Jared was getting ragged around the edges. She couldn't blame him,
but . . .

Karla's gaze drifted to her own reflection. She sighed with relief at the lack of expression on her pale face. She had played the role of impersonal but interested guest for over an hour, ever since they'd arrived at his house. Acting the part was starting to tear at her nerves. So was Jared's behavior. Her eyes skimmed back to his shadowy image in the glass.

Though watching her narrowly, Jared had gone along with her play, giving her the kid-glove treatment ever since she'd whipped by him to exit her apartment. The gloves were wearing a bit thin. Karla recognized the signs. She could feel the confrontation coming. In an attempt to delay the brewing argument, she tried to divert him.

"I can imagine the spectacular view you have from here," she said, sweeping her hand along the window.

"Yeah, it's terrific." Jared's abrupt response dismissed the subject. He moved closer to her, not yet touching, but too close. "Answer my question."

Her spine went rigid. Karla could feel his body heat, scent the tantalizing aroma of after shave and male. Her fingers clutched the delicate stem of the glass she held in one hand, and she slowly inhaled a deep, composing breath. Despite her ploys to forestall it, the moment had come; she couldn't dodge the issue any longer. She had filled the taut silences with compliments on his hilltop house. She had praised the delicious Mexican dinner. She had raved with sincerity about the depth and realistic appeal of the canyon painting hung to advantage above the wide natural-stone fireplace. But she had reached the end of her inconsequential "impersonal guest" chatter rope. Willing defiance into her eyes, Karla met his reflected gaze in the window.

"Yes, I've changed my mind."

"Why?"

Karla felt slightly proud of herself for not flinching at the soft sting in his low voice. She even managed to execute a careless-looking shrug. "I've . . . ah, decided that I really can't spare two weeks away from the gallery fo flit around sight-seeing."

"I don't believe you."

Though she wouldn't have thought it possible, Karla's spine stiffened even more. "Are you calling me a liar?" she asked in a deceptively calm tone.

"Yes."

She shrugged again; this time it didn't look quite as careless. "Believe what you like."

"I always do."

Jared's voice was pitched very low, and yet she heard each individual syllable distinctly, heard and . . . Karla's thoughts fragmented. She'd felt the warmth of his breath on the back of her neck! Her skin prickled, sending responsive quivers down her rigid spine. A sharp sense of warning urged Karla to move, put some distance between them before he—

Too late! The pad of his finger touched down lightly on the spot his breath had sensitized. Karla's stomach muscles contracted against the teasing, arousing sensation caused by the slow movement of his finger, feathering erotically down the curve of her exposed neck.

This was ridiculous! Karla shivered with the thought. He was barely touching her—and she felt as if she were balancing on the edge of a precipice!

Move away from him, dammit!

The order came from the command center deep within her consciousness. Karla wanted to obey, but, as if the lines of communication were snarled somewhere between her head and her feet, her legs refused to work.

Testing, she opened her mouth to see if her voice was still operational.

"Jared"—Karla's voice cracked as his roving finger flicked at the tiny hairs on the nape of her neck. "Please, I wish you wouldn't—" She gasped as his finger flicked again. "Don't do that!" She was unsuccessful at repressing a shiver of response.

"I enjoy touching you," he murmured, slowly lowering his head. "Your skin is so soft, like satin warmed by an open fire." His lips drew near to her tension-taut neck; his warm breath increased her quivering response. "And I know you enjoy it, too."

"No!" Her denial lacked conviction. Karla parted her lips to reinforce her demur, but gasped as the tip of his tongue gently probed the spot his breath had warmed. He flicked his tongue once, twice, with tormenting effect.

"Another lie." There was an underlying harshness in his voice that hinted at growing impatience. "You enjoyed my touch this morning, more than enjoyed it."

Karla shook her head, both in denial and in the hope of discouraging the mind-blanking caress of his mouth. Her action proved fruitless.

"Yes," Jared breathed, tasting her at a maddening, leisurely pace. "I could have taken you right there in your office." His teeth nipped, wrenching a low moan from her compressed lips. "I could have made you mine, anywhere, on your desk, on the floor, even standing upright, against the wall," he insisted softly, deeply.

No . . . No . . . Oh, Lord, no! Unable to shut down her rioting senses, or her hearing, Karla closed her eyes, helpless against the waves of humiliation washing over her. Jared had been deliberately crude. He had hurt her, but the truth in his crudeness hurt her more.

"Stop, Jared . . . Don't . . ." Karla's throat closed, clogged by the tears choking her, tears of shame, tears of remorse, and most bitter, tears caused by a growing fear, not of him, but of her own weakening resistance.

"I must, I want to, I will," he growled, giving proof of Anne's accusation of ruthlessness. His tongue danced in moist swirls, inflicting delicious torture on her skin and sensibilities. "Something happened to change you between the time I left you this morning and the time I came for you this evening." To augment his attack, Jared brushed the tips of his fingers down the length of her arms, causing a tingle from her shoulders to her cuticles. "I don't like the change," he said in a grating whisper. "I want to know what caused it."

Incredibly, Karla felt trapped, ensnared by his tormenting lips trailing over the curve of her neck and the tips of his fingers skimming along her arms. She couldn't move; she couldn't think. Every nerve, every cell in her body shivered in readiness for his command.

He is using you!

The inner scream of warning fought its way from the depths of her instinct for self-preservation, jarring Karla's consciousness awake, activating her defenses.

Concentrating, concentrating, she regulated her breathing process, cooling the heat of desire that was flowing through her veins and melting her will. Karla swallowed, then swallowed again, dislodging the choking tears, allowing a chill to permeate her voice.

"I haven't changed."

"You have." His lips nudged the neckline of her dress aside, then laid claim to her shoulder. "The night of the gallery opening, you were cold and angry. Last night you were cool and contained. This morning you were hot . . . for me." His tongue drew dainty circles on her collarbone. "But tonight . . . tonight you're afraid of me. Why?"

"I'm not afraid of you!" Karla denied, shuddering as his tongue lashed her with silky strokes. "I . . . I am not afraid." Her voice was barely there at all.

Jared laughed. Softly . . . so softly.

The sensuous sound wrapped itself around her, enfolding her in darkness, like a sultry night. Then it pierced her; Karla ached everywhere—in her bones, her skin, her teeth. Her breathing grew shallow. Warm pain spread through her, filled her, releasing her imagination. As if Jared's body had pierced hers, she felt the heat of his possession. The sensation was erotic, glorious . . . and terrifying.

Her resolve liquefying, held captive by his tantalizing mouth and teasing fingertips, Karla stood mute and resistant as Jared removed the wineglass from her limp hand and set it aside. Her eyelids lowered as he trailed his fingers up her arms and gently turned her around to face him.

"What is it?" he demanded in a soft, rasping tone. "Why are you now so afraid?"

"I'm not afraid," Karla insisted, "I . . . I've explained my reason for changing my mind." She was careful to keep her gaze lowered for fear he'd read the lie in her eyes.

Jared didn't need to see into her eyes; he heard the lie in her voice. His fingers curled around the soft flesh of her upper arms. "If nothing occurred to help you change your mind," he began, slowly drawing her quaking body close to his own, "then prove it by agreeing to go with me."

It was a silly challenge; kid stuff, perhaps. Yet, engaged in an inner war between her senses and her common sense, and slightly panicked by the yearning response of her body toward the raw strength of his, Karla was tempted to accept, if only to prove her strength of will to him—and to herself. She was mentally dismissing the temptation as a fool's response, when Jared heaped fuel on the challenge fire.

"You're going to cave in to whatever caused this fear in you," he said, his tone heavy with regret. "You disappointment me. I believed you were made of stronger stuff."

Pride snapped Karla's head up. Anger gave her the momentum she needed to wrench herself from his grasp. Defiance blazed in the eyes she directed at him. "Made of stronger stuff than whom?" she asked with scathing sweetness. "Am I being compared to and judged against one or all of your other"—she smiled unpleasantly—"shall I say, lady friends?"

"Ahh, hah!"

Shaking with an emotion too closely resembling jealousy to be tolerated, Karla lifted her chin and stared at him with cold hauteur. "What, precisely, does 'Ahh, hah!' mean?" she demanded in an ice-coated tone.

"It's an expression conveying understanding," he explained, much too smoothly.

Karla gritted her teeth. "Indeed?"

"Umm."

Fighting an urge to step back, to put some distance between her itching palm and his cynically twisted mouth, Karla inhaled a composure-gathering breath. "May one ask what you now feel you understand?" she asked with hard-found patience.

Jared's reply was blunt and pointed. "You've been listening to the cackle of the gossip hens," he accused. "Was the squawk so lurid in detail, was the scratching so deep, that it either frightened you or filled you with feminine envy of those . . . shall I say, lady friends?"

His speculation was so close to the mark it instilled despair in Karla, despair and doubt. Had she reacted to his apparent ruthlessness or to the account of his numerous affairs? Was she suffering indignation over his arrogant cruelty to his father—and apparently to everyone else who got in his way—or was she smarting at the possibility of being just another female at the end of a long line of willing women?

A sharp, stabbing pain in her chest gave Karla all the answer she required. She felt her skin grow cold, and saw the light of interest gleaming in Jared's dark eyes. Though she hoped he couldn't read her unpalatable thoughts, she was very much afraid that he could.

Detesting the idea of being transparent to him, she clutched frantically at the remnants of her pose of detachment. "Envy?" She raised her eyebrows in a mocking arch. "Why should I feel envious?"

Jared didn't pull his verbal punches, and he didn't hesitate to hit below the belt. "Because they've already enjoyed the pleasure your body lusts after?"

Karla actually felt all the color drain from her face. The remnants of her doubt drained away with it. Oh, he was ruthless in the pursuit of his own way—ruthless and enraging. Her rage was her undoing.

"What an inflated ego you possess," she shot back, speaking without consideration. "I certainly do not lust after you!"

"You could've fooled me," Jared observed very dryly. "In fact you did, just this morning."

The color rushed back into Karla's face. "I . . . I wasn't . . . I didn't— I never—" Her voice, and the blatantly false denial, deserted her.

Jared had the unmitigated gall to grin at her—not just any everyday run-of-the-mill grin, either, but a grin so loaded with sheer male satisfaction it sent Karla's anger to the very edge of the exploding point.

She erupted like a seething volcano. "Why you ... you egotistical paint splasher!" She swept the length of his lean body with a glittering glare of dismissal, so incensed she again rushed into speech before thinking. "You're the last person I'd ever be afraid of being alone with—anywhere!"

Jared's smile was a dead giveaway; she had played directly into his hands. "Bravo," he murmured in congratulations. "I'll make our travel arrangements tomorrow and pick you up at seven the next morning. Okay?"

"Now wait a minute!" Karla exclaimed, suddenly racked by conflicting sensations of dread and anticipation. "I haven't agreed to go with you!"

"Dress comfortably," Jared continued, as if she hadn't uttered a sound of protest. "And please be ready on time. We've got a lot of ground to cover in two short weeks, and I'd like to get started as early as possible."

Damned if she hadn't allowed him to set her up again!

With the stark realization that she had once again walked blindly into Jared's trap, Karla was torn between fury and a pervasive flash of amusement. She ached to administer a blistering put-down, and would have, if she hadn't had to fight the laughter twisting her compressed lips.

No doubt about it: Jared Cradowg was indeed ruthless. He was also extremely clever ... and as sexy as the very devil he appeared to emulate.

He also posed a definite challenge, which Karla, wisely or stupidly, was convinced she had to accept.

Metaphorically, his gauntlet lay at her feet; figuratively, she picked it up with a fatalistic shrug.

"May I have my wine back now, please?" Her tone was reasonable; her voice was revealing.

Retrieving the fragile glass from the table he'd set it upon, Jared offered it to her with a slow smile and a soft question. "You'll be ready at seven?"

Karla hesitated another moment, covering her uncertainty behind the glass she raised to her lips. His intent gaze followed her movement, dark eyes igniting with desire as her mouth touched the platinum-rimmed glass. A responsive shiver ran through her body and alerted her to the very real need to set some ground rules.

"Yes, I'll be ready," she answered slowly, but quickly added, "if you'll agree to a few conditions."

Smiling his approval of her adroit maneuver, Jared inclined his head in a gesture of acceptance. "Name your conditions," he invited expansively.

Fully aware that he could agree to everything and follow through on nothing, Karla eyed him warily and began listing her terms. "First of all, you will take me home tonight as soon as we've reached an agreement."

Jared pulled an injured look. "You don't trust me?"

"I do not," she retorted. "Besides, I've got a lot to do tomorrow, so I'd better have an early night."

"All right," Jared agreed. "What else?"

Karla's features tightened with determination. "When you make sleeping arrangements, you will reserve separate rooms . . . on separate floors, where possible."

"You have a suspicious mind."

"Right." Karla met his reproachful gaze head on.

Jared exhaled a soulful sigh. "Separate rooms. Is there anything else?" He raised his dark eyebrows. "Like separate tables for meals, for example?"

Karla contrived an innocent expression. "Could you?"

"No."

"Pity." Her sigh echoed his. "But then, I suppose that not even you would have the audacity to try seduction in a public restaurant."

"No?" The sensuous smile that curved his mouth caused a mini-explosion deep inside Karla. "I wouldn't make book on that if I were you, sweetheart."

It was utterly preposterous! Karla knew Jared was merely teasing her, and yet she experienced an anticipatory thrill that was frightening by its very intensity.

Advising herself to get a grip on the situation, Karla calmly swallowed the last drops of wine in her glass. She returned his volley as she turned away. "Thanks for the tip; I'll keep it in mind," she said with exaggerated gratitude. "And now I'd like to go home."

"But it's only a little after eight!" Jared exclaimed.

Karla paused, setting her glass aside before glancing at him over her shoulder. "You did agree to take me home, Jared." Her smile mocked him. "Didn't you?"

"Yes, but, ah, don't you have any more stipulations or conditions?"

She slowly shook her head. "Not at the moment." She was amused by his obvious attempt to stall. "But never fear, if I think of any, you'll definitely be the first to know."

Jared's gaze shifted from her to the cluttered table in the dining area to one side of the open living room. "What about the cleaning up?"

A smug smile played over Karla's soft mouth. "I'll leave that chore to you," she said, resuming her stroll toward the door. "It'll give you something to occupy your hands with . . . later this evening."

"I can think of a helluva lot of more pleasurable chores to occupy my hands with," Jared grumbled, reluctantly following her from the house.

"I'm sure you can, and have," Karla replied, tartly. "With any number of willing companions."

"Watch it, honey," he murmured close to her ear as he handed her into the car. "Your envy's showing again."

Recognition of the unvarnished truth fired Karla's anger. Fuming, she held her tongue until he slid behind the wheel, then retaliated with two acid-sweet words. "You wish."

The brute had the nerve to laugh at her. "I know." Sobering, he turned to level a hard stare at her. "I'll gladly admit that my ego is eating your display of resentment like a large serving of dessert, but I'll be damned if I can figure out exactly why you're so touchy about your predecessors."

"Predecessors!" Karla exclaimed, wincing at his calculated use of the plural. By his admission, Jared had confirmed Anne's assessment of his reputation with women. With her mind's eye, she envisioned him, stroking, caressing, *loving* another woman . . . many other women. The vision was unendurable. In an attempt to negate the sick feeling of jealousy stealing through her, she lashed out blindly. "How many women do you need?"

Jared's fingers curled around the steering wheel. "What the hell kind of question is that to ask a man?"

"An honest one!" Karla retorted. Since this appeared to be the night she was doomed to open-mouth, insert-foot, she once again blurted out her feelings without thinking. "Considering your stated intention of having an affair with me, I'm surprised my curiosity surprises you!"

"Well, it does!" Jared snapped. "Look, honey, I know this is supposed to be the enlightened age, where anybody and everybody can let it all hang out, but I don't subscribe to that philosophy. I am not in the habit of discussing my love life." There was a definite warning woven through his controlled tone of voice. "Dammit, Karla, I'm thirty-five years old! Of course there have been other women." He nudged one eyebrow into a peak. "Were you hoping for a virgin?"

"No, I wasn't hoping for a virgin," Karla snapped back at him. "I wasn't hoping, or even looking, for anything!"

"Then what is this all about?"

His question hit a nerve, especially since Karla was beginning to ask herself the same thing. "Nothing," she muttered, inadequately. "Nothing. Your . . . ah, affairs are none of my business."

"That's right, they aren't." Though Jared's response was blunt, his low-pitched voice cushioned the impact of it. "And I realize the right to privacy works both ways." His tone took on a teasing note. "Or hadn't you noticed that I haven't questioned you about your previous lovers?"

"Previous lovers?" Karla nearly choked on the sheer ludicrousness of the expression. But, of course, Jared had no way of knowing how very funny it was. And she wasn't about to set him straight, either. "You haven't even bothered to inquire about the possibility of a *current* lover," she retorted in a cutting tone.

To her amazement, Jared jolted back against the seat as if he'd been struck. "Is there one?" he demanded, in what sounded suspiciously like a feral growl.

"No!" Karla replied at once, unsettled by his show of fierceness. "I certainly wouldn't be here with you now if there were."

"I'm glad to hear it." His movement languid, he raised his hand to glide his knuckles along her jaw, and smiled when he felt her involuntary quiver of response. "I wouldn't enjoy poaching on another man's preserves." His voice had lowered to a raw silkiness that sent a chill skittering down her spine. "For you, I wouldn't hesitate . . . but I wouldn't enjoy it."

"Another man's preserves!" Karla exclaimed, her anger engine revving up. "Another man's preserves! You . . . you—"

His soft laughter drowned her sputtering protest. "Honey, calm down. It was only an expression."

"Damn your macho expressions!" Karla shouted. "'Preserves' implies possession, and I am not, nor will I ever be, any man's possession!"

For an instant, Jared looked startled. Then he sighed. "Oh, shut up, woman." Then, with a deft turn of the hand brushing her jaw, he clasped her chin and tilted her face up to his descending mouth.

As a means of silencing her, his kiss was quite effective.

As a means of arousing her, his tongue was even more so.

Somewhere, in some forgotten corner of her consciousness, Karla knew she should be protesting his means. Yet, somehow, in some mysterious way, she found herself clinging to him, taking from him as much as he was demanding she give.

What she was doing, and allowing Jared to do, was dangerous; she knew it. Karla had believed herself immune to the dangerous lure of the senses. Yet, in an inexplicable way, all of this was somehow comforting.

Could a situation be dangerous and comforting at the same time?

The concept was elusive, dancing just out of reach on the edge of Karla's dwindling comprehension. For an instant, her consciousness engaged in a tug-of-war with her hungry senses; the opponents were unequally matched; the hungry thrill of sensation won, hands down.

The time, place, and circumstances of their sight-seeing trip faded into the nebulous area known as "I'll worry about it later." Reality was encapsulated in the here, the now, and the man . . . especially the man.

And the man was inspiring sensations and feelings within Karla that she had never before experienced. She felt a bone-deep warmth that far exceeded the surface heat generated by the press of Jared's body straining against hers. She felt a security of protection that surpassed the haven of his crushing embrace. She felt a wellspring of emotions that transcended the erotic excitement of his devouring mouth.

Her tremulous senses recognized and identified the feelings that swirled unformed and undefined in her mind. Caught fast in Jared's arms, inside the cramped space of his car, Karla felt as much at ease and at home as she had inside his comfortable and spacious house.

On one level, Karla was savoring the richness and uniqueness of the experience when the bold thrust of Jared's tongue slashed the fabric of all consideration, laying bare the inner core of sensuous response.

Moaning soft, inarticulate sounds of encouragement, she speared her fingers into the thickness of his hair, trembling in reaction to sensations created throughout her body by the glide of the silky strands against her skin. Arching her back, she pressed her body forward as if to pierce his chest with the aching tips of her breasts.

Jared groaned in answer to her soft moans; a dialogue commenced in a language understood only by lovers. His hands sought the arch of her spine, the curve of her waist, the flare of her hip; her fingers skipped a path from the back of his head to the sensitive nape of his neck.

It was heady stuff and arousing play . . . but not nearly, nearly enough. Every living particle and instinct screamed a silent demand for union.

With a muttered curse, Jared tore his mouth from hers and flung his body back against the dubious safety of the door. Stunned and bereft by his abrupt withdrawal, Karla stared at him in confusion and gulped in senses-cooling breaths.

Jared gripped the steering wheel and stared at his knuckles, which were turning white from tension. The taut, silent instant grew into a nerve-racking moment. Within that brief span of time Karla's reason prevailed over her senses, allowing her conscience to waken and react to her surroundings . . . and herself. Heat not at all sensuous in nature rushed to her head, flaming her cheeks, scorching her mind. Appalled at her wanton response to him, Karla stammered into nervous speech. "Jared, I . . . I don't know what to say. I . . ." Her voice failed when he swung around to look at her with a strained expression.

"I have never, ever wanted a woman, any woman, as desperately as I want you right now." His voice was hard and raw with frustration. "Dammit, Karla, what convoluted male-female game are you playing here?"

Karla was struck by his accusing tone as well as by

the content of his angry question. "I'm not playing male-female games!" she exclaimed.

"No?" Jared laughed; the sound produced the same effect in Karla as a nail file being scraped along a rough surface. "Then what the hell was that don't-touch-me act you put on a while ago in the house?" His laughter grew stronger and more grating. "Arrange for separate bedrooms," he parroted her earlier instructions. "On separate floors, where possible."

Karla swallowed with difficulty. "The conditions remain the same, Jared."

He went still, frighteningly still. "If you think I'm going to let you tie me in sexual knots for two weeks the way you did just now, you are out of your beautiful skull!" he snapped. "At each stopover I will reserve one room, which we will share."

Resentment warred with anticipation inside Karla; resentment won. She had allowed one man to manipulate her; she could not, would not, let history repeat itself. Lifting her head, she stared at him with hard-won calm. "In that case," she said coldly, "I will not accompany you." Her muscles clenched defensively as his eyes narrowed, but she forced herself to continue, "Now will you please take me home?"

"Dammit, Karla—" he began in exasperation.

"Jared, please," her soft plea cut across his harsh voice. Turning away from the sight of his glittering eyes and anger-tight mouth, she stared through the side window at the star-spattered night sky. She winced at his muttered curse, then shivered with relief at the reassuring sound of the engine firing to life.

They made the drive to her apartment in absolute silence. Jared drove too fast along the winding, sheer-sided road; Karla clenched her teeth and kept her protests to herself. She was trembling with reaction to the entire evening by the time he brought the vehicle to a screeching stop in front of her building. Anxious to escape, she released her seat belt and groped for the door handle. Jared's rough-edged voice halted her in flight; he already had one foot on the pavement. "You win, Karla."

Her taut body already half out of the car, Karla glanced around at him. "Win?" she repeated. "Win what?"

Jared's mouth tilted into a cynical smile. "You win this game, sweetheart," he said in a tired-sounding drawl. "I'll abide by your conditions."

CHAPTER SEVEN

KARLA DID NOT enjoy a restful night. She was bombarded by too many questions, too many impressions, and far too many doubts to relax, let alone sleep.

Tired and overwrought after the events of the evening, she had given short shrift to her nightly ritual and then crawled into her cold bed, hoping against hope to slip through the escape hatch to unconsciousness. It was not to be. After enduring the mental gymnastics for a while, she tossed back the rumpled covers and left the bed. Her glance settled on her bedside clock as she shrugged into her robe. A resigned groan whispered through her dry lips as the digits pulsed out the numbers 11:59.

"Well, Cinderella," she muttered, wandering listlessly from the bedroom to the small kitchen. "One more minute and your brain turns into a pumpkin."

A self-mocking smile curving her lips, she flicked on the light and padded to the sink.

The content of her rambling words arrested in midair the hand she'd raised to withdraw a glass from the cabinet above the counter.

"Three days."

Karla frowned, no longer even aware that she was talking aloud to herself.

"Three *days*?"

Forgetting the glass of milk she'd thought to use to wash down two aspirin in the hope of reducing the throbbing ache at the back of her head, Karla sank into a chair, narrowed her eyes, and stared into space.

Only three short days had transpired since Karla had first noticed Jared the night of the gallery opening. She expelled a burst of astonished, humorless laughter. It was absolutely unreal! she marveled. How was it possible for a man, any man, to so thoroughly disrupt her entire life in just seventy-two hours? she asked herself in utter bafflement.

Less than ten minutes—and in some cases a good deal less than ten minutes—was required to complete one of the most physically and emotionally draining exercises known to animals, human and otherwise.

The droll thought brought a wry twist to Karla's mouth, and she chided herself for attempting to dodge the issue with facetiousness. But on deeper reflection, she wondered if the spontaneous observation had hit the mark dead center of her problem.

Frowning, Karla carefully picked through her thoughts, connecting them like a child's dot-to-dot puzzle into a discernible pattern. The picture that emerged was not so much that of an insouciant male-female game as it was a battle between the sexes. And, she mused grimly, in this instance "sex" was definitely the operative word.

Though Karla wasn't comfortable with the realization, she had to acknowledge that sexual awareness had crackled between her and Jared from the first words they'd exchanged. For all her denials, she knew that the lure of attraction between them had grown stronger with each encounter.

With a rueful sigh, Karla realized that no matter how adroitly she tried to sidestep the truth, it persisted in staring her in the face and stinging her mind.

The attraction—or chemistry or any other euphemism she could dredge up—was nothing more, and a great deal less, than sheer sexual awareness . . . desire . . . hunger . . . lust.

"No!"

Shoving her chair back, Karla made a last-ditch effort to deny the obvious by running from it. Angrily slapping at the light switch as she rushed by, she fled to her bedroom. But she could not outrun her thoughts.

Desire.

Hunger.

Lust.

The words wreaked havoc with Karla's mind. She had worked too hard, come too far in her determination never again to be vulnerable to any man to surrender without a fight . . . even if her opponent was herself.

Massaging the tension pain in the back of her neck, Karla paced the floor, bombarding herself with questions, raking her abused mind for answers.

What was she to do?

Apply intellect to matter.

How was she to proceed?

In a cool, detached manner.

Why had she agreed to go on a sight-seeing trip with him?

Because he charged her battery.

And there it was—the bald, unvarnished truth. Although Karla didn't particularly like it, she realized she had little choice but to accept it. Now all she had to do was decide how to handle the situation.

Beginning to sway from weariness, Karla slipped out of her robe and into bed. The sheets had grown cold. She shivered, then had to smile at the whimsical thought that swam into her head: She'd be a lot better off if the bed had remained warm and she had grown cold.

But she hadn't, at least, not for very long.

Wincing, Karla shifted uneasily. The chill of withdrawal she had felt steal over her mind and senses on hearing about Jared's reputation for ruthlessness, especially in his use of women, had rapidly changed to melting pliancy and eager participation when she was exposed to the fire of his lovemaking.

Recalling the heat of Jared's blaze, Karla felt herself go all soft and warm inside, outside. Suddenly the bed wasn't cold at all. Her eyes closed slowly as memory stirred, recreating the sensations she'd experienced while locked within Jared's embrace. She stretched her arms up over her head, and her legs moved sinuously. The friction of the sheets against her skin brought an image of Jared's hands, stroking, caressing her thighs. Her chest heaved in a deep, longing sigh. The sound of her expelled breath shattered her reverie.

Her eyes popped open and she groaned aloud in self-disgust. *What was she doing?*

Karla had always been too busy, or too bullheaded— she had never questioned which—to engage in flights of fancy or sexual fantasies about the ideal male. And now, to find herself heaving yearning sighs while wriggling around in bed, fantasizing about Jared Cradowg . . .

Karla jolted into a sitting position, her back straight, her expression militant. With deliberation born of desperation, she forced herself to remember every one of Anne's scathing comments about Jared's coldly conducted affairs. In self-defense, she mockingly told herself that if Jared was a user it was logical to assume he wanted to use her.

But in what way—Karla's mouth slanted wryly as she mused—*besides this obvious one?*

The painting!

The answer slammed into Karla's mind, widening her eyes, hurting her heart. A sick feeling invaded her stomach as she recalled Jared's anger and nastiness when she'd refused to sell the painting to him the night of the gallery opening.

How could she have forgotten? Karla upbraided herself. By his attitude, Jared had made perfectly clear to her his intention to have the portrait. And yet, as far as she could remember, he had not mentioned the subject since then. Karla's eyes narrowed. In point of fact, Jared had neatly ducked the issue when she herself brought it up just that very morning. And tonight his lovemaking had brought her to within a kiss of complete surrender to him, she reflected. Was he hoping to seduce her into happily handing the portrait over to him? she wondered, then supplied what seemed to her the obvious response. Hadn't another man seduced her into handing just about everything of herself over to him? Karla's lips compressed. Wouldn't she ever learn that, with a few rare exceptions like Sean Halloran, the male of the species was a taker?

"That son of a—" Karla ground her teeth in frustration. "Well, Mr. Hot-Shot Artist-cum-Ladies' Man," she muttered, "I think I'll accept your challenge, and we'll see who's in possession of the disputed painting when the two-week jaunt is over."

Her decision made, Karla flopped back on her pillow. A slow smile tugged at her mouth as she settled into her usual sleeping position.

Why not have it all? she asked herself drowsily. Jared had bluntly stated his intention of having two things—an affair with her and the portrait of his grandfather, and it was now obvious he meant to have them in that order. Why not indulge herself by meeting him halfway?

The sparkle of excitement that zigzagged through Karla's body was all the answer she required. She was a mature adult, she reasoned, and a free agent. She had remained celibate for almost seven years, not only by choice but simply because she hadn't met any man who'd generated anything in her but the mildest form of interest. That is, until she had glanced up to see Jared scowling at the painting.

Had it begun then and there? Karla mused, sleepily trying to concentrate. With innate honesty, she had to admit to feeling the simmering attraction to Jared from her first sight of him.

So why not acknowledge that attraction and indulge herself for two weeks? Karla queried herself. She had worked very hard during the past few years. Didn't she now deserve some R&R? Hadn't she earned the right to combine a little pleasure with Jared's suggested business trip?

Yes!

The ringing response reverberated inside Karla's

head. The smile on her lips softened sensuously.

Indeed, why shouldn't she have it all?

It was her last coherent thought before sleep claimed her.

Karla's resolve didn't waver in the cold light of day, nor did her decision weaken as the day progressed. Quite the opposite, in fact; she looked forward to the coming weeks with eager anticipation.

But then, Karla never expected to fall in love.

After ascertaining Anne's willingness to handle the gallery on her own for the two weeks, Karla briefly explained the purposes of the jaunt as research and artifact-buying. Cognizant of her assistant's assessment of Jared's reputation, Karla didn't, of course, burden the younger woman with the additional information that the infamous painter would accompany her as guide . . . and lover. And, considering her inexperience at the game, she fielded Anne's questions with the dexterity and aplomb of a seasoned major-league ball player.

"But when did you get this brainstorm?" Anne asked. "You didn't say a word about it yesterday."

Karla shrugged. "It was a spur-of-the-moment decision." She was relieved she could reply truthfully, since she hated lying and did it badly.

"But why now, all of a sudden?" Anne persisted.

Again Karla was glad that she could give an honest answer. "Because the timing is perfect now, before the volume of business increases after Thanksgiving." She smiled brightly as an idea hit her. "Maybe I can find some unique specialty items for Christmas sales."

Apparently Anne liked the idea, for she returned Karla's bright smile. "You're the boss," she said, indicating the small shop with a flick of her hand. "I'll hold down the fort while you're scouting around. Enjoy yourself."

"Oh, I'm sure I will." Karla laughed, since she had every intention of enjoying herself immensely. So very sure was she, in fact, that she smiled serenely at one point during the day when, upon glancing up at the large canvas, it appeared that the dark eyes in the granite face of Jared's grandfather were staring at her reproachfully.

Her smile twitched whimsically as, staring back at the portrait, she sent a silent message to the spirit of the proud old man, telling him his grandson sorely needed a lesson on the proper way to deal with the modern woman . . . as an equal.

As she smirked at the painting, an odd feeling sent a chill feathering the length of Karla's spine. Unbelievable as it seemed, she had the strangest sensation that the old man had silently replied, telling her she was wrong, and what his grandson sorely needed was not a lesson but understanding, compassion, and love.

Karla stood transfixed for an instant, gazing intently into eyes of black paint that appeared to gleam, not from oil, but with vibrant life. Then she tore her glance away and laughed off the weird feeling.

Muttering, "That kind of silliness is more on Alycia's and Andrea's plane of reality," she turned away, grateful to the customer who walked in at that moment.

To Karla's surprise, Jared neither stopped by the gallery nor called her throughout the entire day and evening. And though she was puzzled by his lack of communication, she assumed he was busy making arrangements. But what surprised her even more was how very much she missed hearing from him. She assured herself that she was relieved Jared hadn't put in an appearance at the gallery, since she felt positive he would speak freely about the trip in front of Anne, but at the same time, Karla couldn't deny feeling abandoned as she spent the long evening hours packing for the trip.

She was ready to leave, her suitcases set neatly along the wall near the door, when the doorbell rang at exactly 6:58 the next morning. After the uneventful evening and a restful night that had been free of conscience-raking and soul-searching, she was astonished by the sudden panic that gripped her. The bell sounded once more, and after drawing a deep, calming breath, Karla squared her shoulders and opened the door.

Attired in tight, stone-washed jeans, scuffed desert boots, a soft chambray shirt, and a denim jacket, Jared looked good enough to wrap in bright paper for a Christmas gift.

Denying an inner hunger for such a gift for herself, Karla smiled and swung the door wide. "Good morning. I'm ready." Her smile dimmed just a smidge. "Even though I must admit that I was wondering if I was engaging in a pointless exercise by getting ready." It was only at that moment that Karla acknowledged the secret fear that had been steadily growing at the edges of her mind, the fear that he had rejected the uncertainty of attempting to seduce her, in favor of the certainty of one of his more accommodating lady friends.

Jared paused, one foot inside the apartment. "Why?" he asked, coming fully into the small entranceway.

Karla lifted her shoulders in a half-shrug, then forced herself to remain motionless while he ran an appraising glance over her. An expression of approval played over his features as he took stock of her cotton shirt, tucked into the belted waistband of tailored olive-green bush pants. He nodded with satisfaction as his gaze noted her sensible canvas walking oxfords.

"When I didn't hear from you yesterday," she replied when he returned his steady gaze to hers, "I thought . . . wondered if you'd changed your mind about going."

"Really?" Jared smiled wryly. "Had you convinced yourself that your conditions discouraged me?" He raised one eyebrow to underline his mocking tone.

Since she hadn't once entertained the idea, Karla could answer with complete honesty; she could even laugh. "No, Jared, I never thought that you'd be put off by anything, least of all my measly strictures."

"Good thing, too, because I never would be," Jared drawled. "As it happens, I had some personal business to take care of," his smile was chiding, "besides making the arrangements in accordance with your conditions."

"You've booked separate rooms?"

He gave her a nod and a dry look. "When I choose to, I follow orders very well."

Karla returned his dry regard with feigned surprise. "You've managed separate dining rooms as well?"

Jared's eyes narrowed. "Don't push your luck, honey." He raised the chiding eyebrow again. "At the risk of sounding trite . . . shall we get this show on the road?"

"You're the tour guide," Karla retorted. "So . . . guide." She turned to scoop up the matching bush jacket she'd draped over her suitcases.

"You'll need that. It's a little cool this morning," Jared said as she slipped her arms into the jacket. "But you'd better bring something heavier for the evenings. It can get cold at night this time of year."

"All right." Karla belted the jacket, then moved to the hall closet to retrieve a down parka. "What about accessories . . . gloves, a scarf, a hat?" she asked over her shoulder.

"I don't think you'll need any of those. Is this all your stuff?"

Karla turned from the closet, the sky-blue parka draped over one arm. "Yes." She frowned as she glanced at the two suitcases he was now holding. "Why?"

"Why?" Jared repeated on a burst of soft laughter. "You amaze me, that's why. We'll be gone for two weeks. I can't think of one woman I know who could manage with less than four very large pieces of luggage for that length of time." He hefted her cases as if they were weightless—which she knew were not. "I do appreciate a woman who travels light."

As compliments go, Jared's was of the garden variety, yet it pleased and warmed Karla. She chatted easily with him through the last-minute check of the apartment, the locking up, and the stowing of her gear in the back of the big four-wheel-drive vehicle.

Finally they were on the road, heading . . . ? "Where are we going?" Karla shifted in the seat to look at him, her expression expectant.

Jared released his visual lock on the congested highway to slant a quick amusement-bright look at her. "You're something else, you know that?"

"In what way?" Karla asked with interest.

His lips curved into a tiny but excitingly sensuous smile. "Well, in a lot of ways . . . but I was referring to the trust you are now placing in me." His wiggled his dark brows and leered in a parody of a silent screen villain. "I could be taking you to my secret hideaway, where you would be at my mercy, helpless while I had my beastly way with you."

Keeping her expression serious, Karla regarded him thoughtfully for a moment, then made a face at him. "Nah," she said, shaking her head. "You have more imagination than that."

Jared's crack of laughter bounced around the interior of the car, then settled in the interior of Karla's heart. "As I said, you're something else," he chuckled. "And your sense of humor ain't half bad, either."

Like his earlier compliment, this one could hardly be described as extravagant, and yet it went directly to Karla's senses. Inordinately happy, she relaxed, fully expecting to enjoy the jaunt. Apparently Jared was experiencing a similar degree of ease, for when he spoke again, his voice held a tone of tranquil camaraderie.

"Would you like me to give you a rundown of the entire two-week itinerary? Or will you settle for a day-by-day outline as we go?"

Karla gave his question due consideration before, on impulse, deciding to be adventurous. "Day-by-day, I think," she replied. "I haven't taken a vacation in years, and I'm in the mood to be surprised."

Jared tossed a smile of approval at her. "Okay, here's the plan for today. We'll drive through the Painted Desert and Petrified Forest National Park. From there we'll go on to the Hubble Trading Post. Our last stop of the day will be at Canyon de Chelly. We'll spend the night there at the Thunderbird Lodge." He glanced away from the road to quirk an eyebrow. "How does that sound to you?"

"Ambitious but interesting," Karla laughed. "Will there be enough daylight hours to see all these places?"

"All except de Chelly." Jared spared a quick glance for her. "Unless we rush through the others, it'll be dark by the time we arrive at the lodge."

Karla began shaking her head before he'd finished speaking. "I don't want to rush through any of it. If you'll remember, the whole point of this trip is to absorb the modern West."

"Right." Jared nodded. "And, considering your notion of the modern West, I think you might be in for the surprise you just said you'd prefer."

Intrigued but confused, Karla frowned. "In what way?"

"I'd rather show you than tell you." Apparently the enigmatic statement was all Jared was prepared to say on the matter, for he immediately changed the subject, catching her off guard with a question from left field. "Why haven't you taken a vacation in years?"

Karla blinked at the abrupt change of topic and blurted an answer without thinking. "Because I didn't have either the time or the money for one."

"I understand." Jared was quiet for a quarter of a mile. Then he sent out another probe. "You were in school during that period?"

This time Karla hesitated, contemplating her response. "Not for the entire period, no."

"So what were you doing to keep yourself too busy and too broke to take a vacation, of even the most inexpensive variety?" he asked with blatant curiosity.

Glancing away to stare at the passing scene of flat yet uneven desertlike terrain, Karla considered telling him her personal life, past or present, was none of his business. Then with a light shrug, she returned her wary gaze to his chiseled profile. "I was keeping myself busy keeping a man," she said with blunt honesty.

Jared's attention was effectively snared. A smile twitched the corners of Karla's mouth at the visible ripple of shock that jolted through his body. Risking disaster, he whipped his head around to stare at her; his expression revealed astonished disbelief.

"You were doing *what*?"

It was almost funny, but as Karla had recently informed her assistant, "almost" didn't count. "You heard me." Her flat tone held not a hint of humor. "And if you don't mind, I'd rather not talk about it," she added, not at all hopeful about deflecting the obvious questions hovering on his lips.

Jared's snort of laughter confirmed her lack of hope. "Not talk about it!" he exclaimed, slanting a lots-of-luck look at her. "You can't toss out a provocative remark like that and then tell me you'd rather not talk about it!"

He was right, of course. Upbraiding herself for having responded to his curiosity in the first place, Karla gazed at his uncompromising profile a moment, then sighed in defeat. "It's a very boring story," she said in warning.

Jared's smile told her plainly that he wasn't buying her evasive ploy. "It'll help pass the miles," he retorted in a mocking drawl.

Asking herself why she continued to walk wide-eyed into his traps, Karla sighed and settled more comfortably into the plush bucket seat. "Well, never say you weren't warned," she muttered. "And remember: Should you find yourself nodding off out of sheer boredom behind that wheel, the life you save may be mine."

"You're stalling."

"You're right."

"Get on with it."

Except for the confidences she had shared with Alycia and Andrea, Karla had never related the humiliating details of her single previous affair. Yet, after a tearing moment of uncertainty, she complied with his command. In a clipped monotone, she recited a brief, concise account of her one and only unromantic romance. When she was finished, she shifted her gaze to the side window in a pretense of utter fascination with the scenery that was in fact so very different from the rolling countryside of her home in eastern Pennsylvania.

Jared had listened to her narrative without interruption. When he did speak, he homed in on one small segment of her account. "Did you say he was your one and only lover?" he asked in disbelief.

Karla turned away from the window to give him a dry look. "Yes, that's what I said. Does that make me some kind of freak or something?"

"You haven't *been* with a man in over five years?"

"Actually, it's been over six years." Karla's waspish tone betrayed her dwindling patience with the subject. "But since I never found *being* with a man all that earth-shattering anyway, I haven't considered myself all that deprived of anything really important."

"Whoa!" Jared ejaculated on a soft burst of grim laughter. "Honey, calm down. That bastard really put you through the shredder, didn't he?" Before she could respond, his voice deepened with compassion, and he went on softly. "The stupid ass injured your emotions, your ego, and your self-esteem!"

His display of concern for her brought a sting of tears to Karla's eyes. Amazed at her emotional reaction, she disguised it with a show of bitter humor. "He didn't do a bad job on my finances, either."

Jared shot a narrow-eyed look at her. What he saw revealed in her face set a muscle jerking in his jaw. His etched features locked into tight lines of determination as he returned his glance to the now nearly traffic-free highway.

"I've upset you, and I'm sorry for that." His voice was low, intense—hardly the tone of a ruthless man accustomed to coldly using women. "But I'm glad you told me and"—he smiled faintly—"at some future time, perhaps, I would like to hear more about your friends, Andrea, Alycia, and Sean. They sound like nice people. I think I'd like them."

The emotional constriction eased in Karla's chest, allowing her to breathe normally. And though the confusion caused by trying to equate this man with the picture Anne had drawn of him remained, she was able to respond without strain. "I think they just might like you, too. And I'll be happy to tell you about them . . . at some future time."

Jared flashed a bone-melting grin at her. "Good enough. I'll look forward to it." He drove off the highway and onto a secondary road. "But, for now, we have arrived at our first destination—the Petrified Forest. Let's relax and enjoy the really *ancient* West."

CHAPTER EIGHT

PONDERING THE EMPHASIS Jared had placed on the word "ancient," Karla glanced around with alert interest. They entered the national park from the south entrance. Jared parked the car at the Rainbow Forest Museum. His reference to the ancient West became clear to her as she examined the museum exhibits of petrified wood and of the area's geological story and human history. Disdaining the explanatory notices posted, Jared proceeded to give her a history lesson.

"This high, dry tableland was once a flood plain," he said in his best tour-guide tones, indicating the entire area with a sweeping movement of one arm. "To the south, tall pinelike trees grew along the headwaters. Crocodilelike reptiles; giant, fish-eating amphibians; and small dinosaurs lived among a variety of plants and animals that we know today only through fossils."

They moved slowly from one exhibit to another as Jared spoke, and though Karla's eyes were fastened to the displays of multicolored petrified wood and the conceptual paintings of the animal, plant, and tree life of that long-ago time, her ears were sharply attuned to his deep voice.

"The trees fell and were washed by swollen streams into the flood plain," Jared continued as he ushered her through a door at the back of the museum. "There they were covered by silt, mud, and volcanic ash, and these deposits cut off oxygen, slowing the decay of the logs. Gradually," he went on, leading her onto the trail through a section named Giant Logs, "silica-bearing waters seeped through the logs, replacing the original wood tissues with silica deposits. As the process continued, the silicas hardened, preserving the logs as petrified. That all happened about two hundred million years ago," Jared said, inclining his head toward the huge pieces on the ground, which looked like brilliantly hued tree trunks but felt like stone.

"Two hundred million years!" Karla exclaimed, stooping to examine the pieces more closely.

"Yes." Jared smiled. "This is ancient, yet still an integral part of the modern West."

From the museum, they followed the twenty-seven-mile scenic drive through the park. Jared stopped at several pullouts, and they left the car to wander around, Karla exclaiming enthusiastically over the abundance of petrified trees. But it wasn't until he had parked in one area that Karla once again felt the impact of his reference to the ancient West.

Carrying binoculars he'd taken from the glove compartment, he led her to a railed section of what appeared to be rock that jutted over a shallow canyon. Strewn on the canyon floor were enormous rocks. Pointing out the side of one such rock, Jared told her to focus the glasses on its flat side. For a few minutes, Karla could see nothing but a blur of slate gray. Then, as the blur cleared, she gasped.

Since he had not given her time to read the explanatory sign posted near the car park, the petroglyphs were a delightful surprise.

"How wonderful!" Karla exclaimed, moving the glasses slowly as she examined the ancient paintings.

"I thought you'd like it," Jared observed dryly. "It's called Newspaper Rock. Very little is known about it, other than that it is thousands of years old"—he smiled —"but, again, definitely part of the modern West."

"A fantastic part," Karla agreed, sparing a quick glance away from the sight to return his smile. "The paintings of the different animals are incredible!" she said, focusing on the likeness of a large wildcat. After looking her fill, she gazed up at him, her expression contemplative. "What were they like, I wonder, the people who left those drawings?"

"I've wondered the same," Jared said, "and drawn my own conclusions." He laughed. "The beauty of it is that my speculations can't be either proved or disproved."

After a moment's consideration, Karla realized that he was right. She laughed with him. "And what conclusions have you drawn?" she asked, resisting an urge to focus once more on the fascinating Newspaper.

Jared didn't resist a similar urge. Plucking the glasses from her hand, he stared through them intently at the rock face. "I suspect they weren't all that much different from us. Whether deliberately or not, they left a legacy for the future on the rock." He grinned as he lowered the glasses. "Hell, for all we know that intriguing rock face might have been their graffiti wall." The intensity of his stare didn't lessen as he transferred it to her eyes. "Yes," he murmured, "I suspect they were very much like us; they laughed, they cried, they loved, they lived out their years—good, bad, or indifferent—and then they died"—he sighed—"and very likely, questioned every feeling and emotion along the way . . . just as we more sophisticated humans do today, thousands of years later."

Karla had been attentive to his every word, and when he finished, she simply stared at him, attempting to equate the philosophic man before her with the ruthless user Anne had described to her. The exercise was not unlike trying to arrive at the sum of three by adding one and one. Karla wasn't dull or stupid, and it didn't take long to conclude that there was an unknown factor in the equation of Jared Cradowg—but then, she mused, wasn't there usually an unknown factor in any complex personality? A frown was beginning to pucker her brow when Jared's wry voice derailed her train of thought.

"Why do I have this sensation of being dissected?"

Karla started and felt her face grow warm as she gazed into his dark eyes, gleaming with amusement. "I'm sorry, I didn't mean to stare." She lowered her eyes, then immediately looked up at him again. "I was thinking about what you said." The frown returned to her brow. "Do you view all of history in such a personal way?"

Jared smiled, not condescendingly, but with a warmth that Karla felt to her very depths. "I view history in terms of lives lived, if that's what you mean—lived and relived through all the necessary phases of growth and development."

Karla was suddenly uneasy; his explanation had the ringing echo of similar theories expounded by Andrea, Alycia, and the celebrated historian, Sean Halloran. And since the concept had strong overtones of lives lived repeatedly, in ongoing cycles of awareness, she was uncomfortable with it. Like many others, Karla was thoroughly steeped in the now, today, and had firmly proclaimed she had no time to indulge in the esoteric possibility of recurring experiences.

And this was the man she had decided she'd have an affair with?

The thought was sobering, and it demanded some serious consideration. Automatically, she began walking beside him when Jared turned to stroll back to the car. Awareness rushed back to her with the electric tingle that charged up her arm and through her body when he casually took her hand and laced his fingers through hers. Her lips forming a soundless *O*, Karla raised her startled eyes to his.

"You object?"

Object? Karla shivered. How in the world could she object to a touch that, though ordinary, felt so deliciously exciting, so very right? She couldn't, and told him so. "No, I don't object."

"Good."

Again the ordinary, and yet his response described the feeling settling inside her. With a sense of shock, Karla realized that the very ordinary act of clasping hands with Jared had instilled in her a deeper sense of excitement and satisfaction than she had ever experienced—even while in the supposed throes of the physical expression of love. The realization sparked a related consideration: If merely holding hands with Jared could induce such pleasure, what would making love with him be like?

Simultaneously aroused and frightened by the prospect, Karla slid a sideways glance at Jared, to discover him studying her intently. He was quiet, allowing her thoughts to bounce around wildly, until they were seated in the car. Then he somehow managed a frown and a smile at one and the same time.

"There's a problem?"

A problem? Karla had to fight down a burst of apprehensive laughter. At that moment, she felt she had almost as many problems as the forest had petrified trees, the primary one being her own amazing emotional and physical reaction to the many-faceted man seated beside her.

Her resolve of the night before had seemed perfectly clear and simple: She would take some time off, which was long overdue in any case, and enjoy Jared's company and the combined research and sight-seeing jaunt. Now, suddenly, her decision didn't seem at all simple; the picture that Jared was presenting to her of himself was too interesting, too intelligent . . . and too damned appealing.

Karla felt vaguely threatened, but she couldn't pinpoint exactly why she felt as she did. So, naturally, she pounced on the single unnerving statement he'd made to her.

"I am having a bit of a problem with your reference to lives lived *and relived* through all the necessary phases of growth and development."

"You know precisely what concept I was referring to," he retorted with a soft, chiding laugh.

"That's what I was afraid of." Karla groaned. "Your ideas sound too much like those expounded by Andrea and Alycia, and even Sean, at times." She sighed.

Jared laughed. "I knew from the little you said that there was a reason I felt I'd like your friends! They're into esoteric studies?"

"In spades." Karla rolled her eyes. "Even though, most of the time, they're quite normal."

"What's normal?" Jared demanded, shrugging his shoulders. "Can you define normalcy?"

Feeling cornered, Karla retaliated. "Well, it's certainly not the belief in lives lived—and relived— through all the necessary phases of growth and development!"

His smile started slow, and grew into a wicked grin. "You have factual proof of that, do you?"

Beginning to get annoyed, Karla glared at him. "You know I don't. But then, you don't have proof to back up your belief, either, do you?"

"No, but I'm not demanding or seeking proof." Jared's tone was free of concern. "I neither accept nor reject the concepts. I have an open mind, and I find the possibilities fascinating . . . especially one particular recent theory."

"And that is?" she asked warily.

"The theory of soul mates being drawn successively to each other," he replied quietly. "I feel the pull of the drawing force, and I think you feel it, too."

Soul mates! Karla was stunned and shaken . . . and suddenly very uncertain of every earthbound precept she harbored within herself. Soul mates. The term activated a humming response deep inside her. She didn't like it, but she couldn't deny it; she also felt the pull of the drawing force.

It was a strong physical attraction, nothing more, she told herself.

Acting on the defensive thought, Karla shook her head and repeated it to him. "What we feel is a strong physical response to each other, Jared. There isn't anything esoteric about that."

"You're grasping at straws, sweetheart, and you know it."

The calm certainty of his voice set loose a flood of conflicting emotions in Karla, uppermost of which was the thrill of pleasure she felt at his sincere-sounding endearment. As she had before, Karla lashed out at him without thinking.

"I'm in lust, Jared!"

"I'm in love, Karla."

Full stop. Shut down. Experiencing the odd sensation of mental abrogation, Karla stared at Jared with blank astonishment as the impact of his declaration shuddered through her entire system. When reason asserted itself, it did so with a rush of internal dialogue.

Love. The man had said he was in love with her. Hadn't he? Yes, he had. But why? He couldn't be in love with her. Could he? No. It wasn't possible. They were still virtual strangers. They barely knew each other. They hadn't even been to bed together! It wasn't possible. Was it? Well, maybe . . .

"Have you been petrified like these ancient trees?" Jared asked, effectively ending her inner argument.

Karla blinked, then shivered and attempted a laugh that sounded more like a sob. "I don't believe this!" she cried, glancing around convulsively. "I'm sitting in the middle of a national park . . . and Jared! I simply don't believe this!"

Jared's smile was so tender it made her want to cry. "Don't let it throw you, sweetheart. You'll get used to the idea." His glance tracked hers. "But for now, we'd better get moving." Settling in his seat, he switched on the ignition. "We'll talk about it later." As he drove out of the parking area, he shot a rakish grin at her. "Tonight," he promised, "when we're alone."

The remainder of the day was predictably anticlimactic. Feeling mind-bruised and emotion-numbed, Karla was only vaguely aware of the sights the park had to offer. Though she voiced appreciation and awe of the magnificent shadings of purple, red, and gray sediments that streaked the eerie moonscape mounds of the Painted Desert, and exclaimed excitedly over the skeleton of Gertie, the German shepherd—size plant-eating plateosaur, the world's oldest dinosaur skeleton, discovered near Chinde Point in 1985 and being assembled in the park by paleontologists, Karla really didn't absorb much of it. Nor did she eat or absorb much of her lunch in the Visitor Center restaurant.

The minimal amount of activity her mind did engage in was centered on Jared's unexpected and amazing avowal of love and his promise of more of the same that evening. In consequence, Karla said very little. Jared, on the other hand, kept up a running commentary, all of it impersonal and pertaining to the sights and terrain.

It was somewhere between the national park and their next stop at Hubbell's trading post that a suspicious idea wormed its slithery way into Karla's swamplike consciousness. Jared himself sparked the idea with a wry remark.

"I'm relieved you're no longer afraid of me the way you were the other night."

"I was never afraid of you!" Karla denied indignantly.

Jared blessed her with his tender smile. "Yes, darling, you most assuredly were."

Not feeling equal to a heated argument, Karla contented herself with glaring at his complacent profile before turning to stare out the side window at the looming rock mountains dotting the desert landscape and, after they were inside the Navajo reservation, frowning in confusion and wonder at the mound-shaped structures set a short distance from practically every dwelling. It was while she was staring, frowning, and fuming that the idea wriggled into her mind.

At their second meeting, Jared had stated unequivocally that they would have an affair. Two nights ago, he had reached the conclusion—with reason—that she was somewhat emotionally afraid of him. A few hours ago, Jared had suddenly proclaimed his love for her. Could there be a connection between his prediction and her fear? Karla asked herself. What do you think? her self answered.

I think I'd better think about this.

And think Karla did. She pondered deep and long, all through her outward display of interest in Hubbell's, a national historic site and the oldest continually active trading post on the Navajo reservation.

While she smiled and talked with the attractive Navajo park ranger, reacting enthusiastically to the post's separate small rooms, which contained groceries and dry goods as well as traditional hand-wrought jewelry and intricately patterned rugs, Karla speculated on the motives of the tall, ruggedly handsome man ambling along beside her, looking as Indian as the young woman, but in a different, more chiseled way.

Impatiently ignoring the quivering excitement merely walking by his side generated within her, Karla examined the possibility of Jared ruthlessly using the words of love to disarm her, leaving her too weak to resist his desire to use her in the physical act of love. Though her reflections caused considerable pain in her mind and body, Karla was forced to conclude that, in light of what Anne had told her, her supposition was more probable than possible.

Hurting with a depth she had never before experienced, and was afraid to examine too closely, Karla avoided looking at Jared. Instead, she concentrated on the tour of the outbuildings off to one side of the post and assured herself that the hot sting in her eyes was caused by the glare of the afternoon sunlight.

Gratitude washed through her when the ranger led them into the house behind the post, which had been the residence of the post's founder, John Lorenzo Hubbell. The interior was dim and shadowy, giving her a reasonable excuse for blinking. Confined within expanding waves of misery, Karla gave up all pretense of alert interest, shifting her gaze dully, from the array of furniture to the paintings on the walls as the ranger described them.

"Are you all right?"

The low, concerned sound of Jared's voice close to her ear nearly caused Karla to stumble over the threshold as they exited the building. Averting her eyes, she nodded her head and silently cursed the renewed need to blink.

"I'm fine. Just getting a little tired, I guess." Karla winced inside at the reedy sound of her own voice. "I . . . ah," she flashed an unconvincing smile his way without actually looking at him. "It's . . . umm, rather hot for November, isn't it?" she asked raggedly, too brightly.

"Not for Arizona," Jared replied. "It's pleasantly warm, but if you think the sun's hot today, wait until you're exposed to its relentless heat in mid-August."

"If I survive that long." Karla didn't realize she'd muttered the thought aloud until Jared responded to it.

"You *are* tired. Let's go," he said, reaching for her hand. "I think you've had enough sight-seeing for one day."

A sensation not unlike panic gripped Karla with the feel of his palm gliding over hers, and she was forced to impose every ounce of willpower she possessed to keep from snatching her hand away from his. It was crazy, incredible, but it was fact nonetheless: Karla was electrified and completely undone by the devastating effects of Jared's touch.

Suffering agonies of pleasure from the feel of his skin imprinting itself on hers, and feeling herself as firmly captured as her fingers entwined with his, Karla moved with him when Jared began walking toward the car. Then, when necessity dictated that he release her, she felt abandoned and bereft.

Emotional exhaustion slammed into Karla as Jared drove away from the trading post. Suddenly tired of thinking, speculating, and attempting to figure Jared out, she rested her head against the back of the seat and shut her eyes. A soft sigh whispered through her lips. Later she'd think about her suspicions, her emotions, her odd feeling of anguish, she promised herself, pushing the questions and doubts to the edges of her consciousness. For the moment, all she wanted, longed for, was forgetfulness and rest.

Karla was asleep before they reached the main highway.

The cessation of motion woke her. Starting, she sat

upright and glanced around in confusion. There wasn't much for her to see. Dusk had surrendered to night. Lights illuminated the entrance doors of the building before which the car was parked, and dimmer lights flickered along the narrow streets of a small community. Beyond their glow, darkness cloaked the landscape. She was alone in the car. Even as she began to frown, wondering where Jared had gone, she saw him push his way out through the lighted entrance doors. A warm smile curved his mouth when he saw that she was awake.

"Feel better?" he asked, after sliding behind the wheel. "Rested and ready for dinner?"

"Yes to both questions," Karla answered, her vague smile revealing her feelings of confusion and disorientation. "Where are we?"

Jared fired the engine before replying. "This is the Thunderbird Lodge at Canyon de Chelly." He gestured to indicate the area, then drove down one of the streets that led to rows of motel units. He brought the car to a stop in the last parking space in the row. "This is it," he said, inclining his head toward the units. "We have the two end rooms."

Jared allotted the inside room to Karla, carried her luggage inside for her, then stood beside her as she took stock of her surroundings.

"What do you think?" he prompted.

The room was an adequate size, not luxurious but pleasant, comfortable-looking, and clean. "It's very nice," Karla said, crossing the floor to peek into the bathroom. She arched her eyebrows as she turned away from the doorway. "Is there a restaurant?"

"A cafeteria." Jared smiled—somewhat apologetically, she thought—and shrugged. "It's not fancy, but it's clean, and the food is good."

Karla regarded him solemnly. "I don't need fancy, Jared . . ." She hesitated before continuing, "I can be perfectly content with good." Fully aware that her claim could be taken in several different ways, she waited, praying he wouldn't give an obvious response. She was still trying to cope with the tensions of the day and too emotionally jangled to field sexual innuendos.

Staring at her thoughtfully, Jared answered her prayers. "I'm glad you're not disappointed." He shot a glance at his watch. "It's six-ten now and the cafeteria closes at eight-thirty. Can you be ready in an hour?"

Karla gave him an arch, superior look. "If necessary, I can be ready in fifteen minutes flat . . . but I'm longing for a long, hot shower, so I'll take the full hour, thank you."

The echo of Jared's appreciative laughter haunted her long after he strode from the room.

The cafeteria was everything Jared had said it was— and wasn't. The large room was clean, bright, and functional; it was not in any way elegant. The food was hot, solid fare, filling and delicious; it was not gourmet cuisine.

Karla was satisfied with the place and the meal . . . for several reasons, the principal one being that it was definitely not conducive to seduction. Though the shower and a fresh, if suitcase-crumpled, change of clothing had helped boost her flagging spirit, she was still undecided about how she was going to react to whatever form of seduction Jared was planning to use.

The restaurant's ambience or, more accurately, the lack of it, greatly eased the remaining threads of apprehensive strain knotting her nerves. While showering and dressing, she had looked forward to a soothing glass of wine to accomplish the easing process, but Jared dashed her hope of that notion when she mentioned it to him as they'd strolled from their rooms to the cafeteria.

"You're going to have to make do with coffee or a soft drink, at least through dinner," he'd said enigmatically. "We're on the reservation, and liquor is not allowed."

Though she silently questioned the fairness of the stricture, Karla made do with coffee. But throughout the meal she pondered the meaning of his phrasing. It became clear after they returned to their rooms.

All the tension, apprehension, and strain Karla had temporarily released during dinner slammed back into her as they walked to their rooms through the brisk fall air. Beyond the lights in the large compound, the night was as dark as her thoughts. Within the minutes required to return to their rooms, she was flooded by all the questions and conflicting emotions she'd been mentally sidestepping ever since she had escaped into sleep in the car.

Karla fully expected Jared to make his move on her once they were alone, and she had no idea how she was going to respond to his advance. She wanted to run and hide, but acknowledged that it was much too late in the game to retreat. She was fearfully uncertain of her ability to carry through on the decision she had made with arrogance in the safety and privacy of her apartment. She was running scared . . . but she had run out of time.

Jared had been unusually quiet and reticent during dinner, leaving Karla to wonder what he was thinking . . . planning. He was silent as they walked back to their rooms. Karla had no idea what to expect from him, but it certainly wasn't the rejection she received when he turned and walked away from her an instant after unlocking and opening her door.

Numb with surprise, Karla watched him disappear into his own quarters. Then she took a few steps into her room, tossed her jacket on a chair, and came to a dead stop, the door wide open behind her. A frown tugged her eyebrows together. She had been preparing herself to jump in any one of several directions. Having the need to do so pulled out from under her like a scatter rug left her immobilized and stunned. A devastating sense of rejection seared through her, blazing a path for the anger that followed. Of all the emotions Karla had geared herself to contend with, the pain of rejection had never even entered into the picture. The anger expanded—anger at herself for her unrealistic expectations, anger with Jared for deliberately instilling them then ruthlessly snatching them away.

Hell, he hadn't even wished her a good night! The indignant thought had no sooner formed in her mind than Karla heard the quiet click of the door being shut, immediately followed by the low, attractive sound of Jared's voice.

"Ready for that glass of wine?"

Whirling around, Karla stared at him, her expression changing from consternation to astonishment. In one hand he held an uncorked bottle of what she recognized as a fine, expensive white wine, in the other he held two ordinary motel-room glasses. Assimilating the realization that she hadn't been rejected, she shifted her confused gaze from the bottle to the glasses.

"I thought you said that stuff"—she inclined her head at the bottle—"wasn't allowed on the reservation."

Jared smiled in a way that did strange and exciting things to her senses, things more potent and intoxicating than the contents of the bottle he tipped over the glasses.

"There's no law that I know of against bringing your own," he said dryly, holding one of the glasses out to her.

Karla automatically reached for the glass, but she didn't immediately sip from it to test the quality of the golden liquid. She was too busy testing the quality of the dawning comprehension shimmering through her.

Of all the expectations Karla had nurtured, the absolute last one she had considered was the possibility of falling in love. Yet, in that instant, there it was, staring her in the face, in the form of the tall man standing less than four feet away from her.

Staring at him with heightened awareness, Karla suddenly felt cold and hot, frightened and exhilarated. Conflict dissolving, she absorbed him with her activated senses.

He had removed his jacket and was dressed casually in a fine-knit pullover, faded jeans, and soft leather moccasins, without socks. His loose-limbed stance was as casual as his attire. But there was nothing casual about his eyes. His eyes were dark and watchful, and held a hint of uncertainty. That flicker of uncertainty robbed her of her last hope of defense. Sighing softly in surrender, she accepted the inevitable. The admission came hard, but it would not be denied.

Karla was hopelessly in love with Jared Cradowg.

CHAPTER NINE

"KARLA, SWEETHEART, WHAT'S wrong?" The sharp concern in Jared's voice brought Karla out of her trancelike introspection. "You're trembling and pale. Are you feeling sick?" He walked to her to take the glass from her unsteady hand. "Honey, tell me!" he insisted. "What is the matter with you?"

"Nothing!" Karla blurted out between gasps of senses-restoring breath. Since the threat of physical torture wouldn't have made her admit to him her mentally torturing revelation, she was reduced to gazing at him with pleading eyes; and even she wasn't sure of exactly what she was pleading for.

In any other circumstances, Jared's uncharacteristic reaction might have been both enlightening and amusing. His expression could only be described as near panic-stricken; his eyes were very dark, shadowed by concern. He seemed suddenly unsure of what to do—not at all like the confident, arrogant man Karla knew him to be. The edge of authority always present in his voice had given way to a tone of tender care, underlined by desperate vigilance.

"Dammit, something's wrong." Balancing both glasses in one broad hand, Jared slid his arm around her waist and gently drew her quivering body to his, as if to protect and support her with his strength. "Come sit down," he said in a soft tone of inducement. He led her to the bed, and after they were seated side by side on the edge of the mattress, he murmured coaxingly, "Talk to me, my love. Tell me what's wrong."

His demeanor was at once baffling and endearing. Already weak with the acknowledgment of the love she felt for him, Karla's last shred of resistance and doubt dissolved in the hot moisture that rushed to her eyes. Gone was her cool decision to indulge herself in a purely physical short-term relationship with him, replaced by a yearning to be all and everything to him.

His love. He had called her his love, and Karla was in an agony of need to be the object of his love, not merely another partner in passion. But the passion was there as well, heating her senses, firing her imagination, creating an emptiness deep within her.

"Karla! Will you talk to me?" Jared's tone was now teetered on the fine line between impatience and gathering panic. "Tell me what is—" He broke off, eyes narrowing. "You're afraid again, aren't you?" he demanded on a harshly exhaled breath.

Karla smiled and took her glass from his no longer rock-steady hand. "No, Jared, I'm not afraid." She sipped the wine and stared directly at him over the rim of her glass. She was calm now, resigned to the realization that she would accept whatever of himself he wished to give.

"Well, what is it, then?" He took a deep swallow from his own glass. "Are you feeling sick or excessively tired?"

"No." Karla hid a wry smile behind her glass as the thought whispered through her mind that she could hardly tell him she felt excessively aroused.

Why couldn't she? Her smile faded at the follow-up thought. *What, other than her own reticence, was there to prevent her from telling him precisely what she was feeling?*

"Well, then, what—" Jared began.

Consigning reticence to hell, Karla quietly interrupted him. "I need to be with you, Jared."

"What?" He whispered the single word, then went deathly still, his eyes revealing the conflict of hope and uncertainty he was experiencing.

Though fascinated by it, Karla didn't have the heart to let him dangle over the pit of sensual suspense. Plucking up her courage, she repeated boldly, "I need to be with you." She set her glass aside, then brought her hand to his face. "Make love with me, Jared."

"Oh, Karla," he breathed, lifting his hand to hers. "I need you, too." Leaning around her, he set his glass on the nightstand next to hers. As he straightened, he simultaneously slid one hand from hers in a tantalizing line to her shoulder, while gently clasping her other shoulder with his free hand. "You can't imagine how very much I need you."

Her senses quivering with anticipation, Karla watched and waited breathlessly as he slowly, slowly, lowered his mouth to hers.

Jared's kiss was well worth the wait, and utterly different from the others they had shared. With the touch of his mouth to hers, Karla felt a piercing sweetness unlike anything she had ever before experienced. Tender, warm, tentative, his lips caressed hers, igniting within her a hunger that swiftly expanded into a raging desire for more.

Reacting without a qualm to the immediacy of her response, Karla parted her lips in invitation, curled her arms around his neck, and moaning low in her throat, drew him with her as she fell back onto the bed. Her mouth trembled with anticipation as she felt his lips move against hers.

"Slowly, love, slowly," Jared murmured. "Though the need is great, I don't want to rush." He paused to glide the tip of his tongue along her lower lip. "I want to savor our first time together."

"But I want—" Karla began a whispered protest, only to be silenced by his mouth.

"And I want you," Jared said on a ragged breath as he raised his head. "And I mean . . . *you*." A flare of emotion sparked in the depths of his eyes. "I don't want a quick, marginally satisfying roll between the sheets, Karla," he explained when she expressed confusion over his meaning. "I want to be with you, kiss you, caress you, tremble with anticipation as you caress me. I want to draw our lovemaking out until I'm ready to scream or beg to be inside you."

Through the haze creeping over her consciousness, Karla concluded that Jared was an even greater artist than she'd imagined. She was already trembling in response to the erotic pictures he was drawing in her mind with his passionate words. Rendered pliant, willing to comply with any and everything he might desire of her, she smiled with unpracticed sensuousness. "I want that, too."

Jared swallowed with visible difficulty and, in so doing, turned Karla's insides to liquefied jelly.

"I want to see you . . . all of you."

"Yes."

"I want you to see me . . . all of me." He drew a breath and held it.

"Yes." Karla slid her arms from around his neck and set to work on the top button of her blouse. Her fingers stilled when he covered them with his hand. She raised startled eyes to his.

"Let me, love," he pleaded, dipping his head to brush his parted lips over hers.

Pushing himself away from her with exciting reluctance, Jared stood, then drew her up to stand facing him. Then, with excruciating slowness, he unfastened the small buttons on her blouse and slid it off her shoulders. The glide of his palms over her skin ignited fires that burst into tiny tongues of flaming desire. The flames licked hungrily in the wake of his hand with each successive piece of cloth he eased from her trembling body.

By the time Karla stood before him, unadorned and unafraid, her body was a shimmering torch, glowing from within with excitement and blazing with readiness for the quenching fire of his possession.

"You're beautiful." Jared's voice contained hushed reverence. "So very beautiful." His gaze locked with hers, he grasped the hem of his pullover. Karla halted his move by placing her hands over his.

"Let me . . . love."

The disrobing process was repeated. Thrilling to the texture and feel of each newly exposed portion of his magnificent masculine form, Karla mirrored his action precisely. Her eyes flickered and widened as the last article of clothing to be removed revealed to her the impressive strength and power of his need for her.

"You're beautiful, too," she said in an awed whisper as, hesitantly, she stroked him delicately with her trembling fingertips.

"Dear God!" Jared groaned, shuddering in response to her touch. "Karla..." Clasping her hand, he drew her with him onto the bed. "Love me. Let me love you."

His mouth found hers; his tongue plunged with a desperate hunger. Karla's mind and body surrendered to ever increasing, deepening waves of pleasure.

Love given and received.

Jared allowed long, intoxicating minutes to unwind while cherishing every inch of her body with his hands. Karla had never felt so tenderly cherished; the sensation was shattering. Tears glistened to the ends of her eyelashes and drowned the words of love that rushed to her throat.

"Why are you crying?" Alarm momentarily banished the passionate huskiness in Jared's tone. "Have I hurt you in some way?"

"No!" Karla was quick to reassure him. "I'm not really crying. It's just that I..." She gently smoothed the frown from his brow. "Jared, I never believed it could be this beautiful. I never knew." Her voice deserted her; Karla let her caressing fingers express her feelings.

Jared kissed her fingertips as they outlined his lips. "I'm glad you never knew, and grateful I'm the one to make it beautiful for you." He kissed her mouth with breathtaking tenderness that quickly exploded into devouring hunger. With his mouth and tongue, he created a heat that scorched her lips and dried her tears.

More passionately aroused than she would have ever imagined possible, feeling freer than ever before in her life, Karla blazed an exploring trail of her own, returning touch for touch, caress for caress, deep probing kisses for even deeper, more probing kisses. Tension spiraled and coiled inside her until, unable to bear another empty moment, she gasped his name and arched her body in silent supplication.

Granting her plea, Jared eased his taut body into the cradle of her thighs. A thread of amusement was woven through his tightly strung voice. "How did you know I was ready to plead for you?"

"Because I've been biting my lip against the same plea for what seems like forever." Karla returned his amusement with simple honesty.

He bent to kiss her. "I know it has been some years since you've been like this with a man. I won't hurt you, my love," he promised. "I'd die first."

Tears gathered in her eyes again; she smiled and blinked them away. "I know you won't." With those four words, Karla knowingly committed her body, her emotions, her trust, and her love into his safekeeping.

Moving slowly and with exquisite care, Jared consciously claimed possession of her body, unknowingly taking possession of her soul as well. Karla gave both joyously, crying out his name softly when, sliding off of the cutting edge of almost unbearable pleasure and tension, her body shuddered with pulsating release.

Jared's loving cry of satisfaction echoed her own.

* * *

The day was bright; the sun was warm; Karla was content to the bone and blissfully happy. Unwilling to look for dark clouds on their horizon, she pushed all her questions and doubts about Jared's motives to the back of her mind with her fears for the future as she smiled at him over the breakfast table.

"What's on the agenda for today?" she asked, reminding him of his promise to give her a day-to-day briefing.

Jared's expression and smile were happy and free from strain. "De Chelly, of course," he said, referring to the canyon a short distance from the lodge. "Since there are no tours into the canyon during the fall and winter months, we'll have to be satisfied with viewing it from the rim. From here, we go on to Monument Valley, and from there to Lake Powell, where we'll spend the night." He arched his eyebrows. "Sound okay?"

"Sounds fine," Karla agreed, thinking: especially the spend the night part. A secret little smile twitched her kiss-softened mouth.

Though Jared frowned, the laugh lines at the corners of his eyes creased, betraying inner amusement. "What's so funny?" he demanded in an unconvincing growl.

"Why, nothing." Karla tried to control her lips and look innocent; she failed in both.

"Karla, I want to know why you're wearing that intriguing smile." His voice was low with warning.

Karla was no longer impressed—at least, not with his display of ferociousness. The going was slow, but she was learning about him. And, surprisingly, one of the things she had learned was that behind the fierce facade Jared affected was a very gentle, rather shy man.

The knowledge gave her strength and hope . . . and the courage to tell him the truth. "I'm smiling in anticipation."

"Of what?" He narrowed his eyes, but was unsuccessful at hiding the expectation flaring in the dark depths.

"Tonight."

Karla held her breath, waiting for his reaction; it was stunning. Before her shock-widened eyes, the supposedly ruthless Jared Cradowg fell apart. He didn't move a muscle; his expression didn't change by as much as a flicker, and yet Karla was witness to the effect of her honesty on him; his eyes reflected the crumbling of his inner barriers. Acting on her intuition, she reached across the table to cover his hand with her own, offering understanding and encouragement.

Jared's blunt eyelashes flickered. His gaze dropped to her hand resting on his. Then he slowly raised his eyes to hers and turned his hand to meld their palms together in an unspoken request for bonding. Without hesitation, Karla granted his plea with the symbolic act of twining her fingers with his.

The significance of the moment was not lost on either of them. For an eternity of an instant, the world and all its attendant problems receded, leaving Karla and Jared alone, yet as one in spirit, in a unity more intense and binding than could ever be achieved by a mere physical blending of bodies.

The magic of the instant was shattered by the loud crash of a coffee cup a waitress accidentally knocked to the floor. Karla and Jared blinked, then smiled in unison.

"You feel ready for the canyon?" he asked, tightening his grasp on her hand before releasing her.

"I feel ready for anything." The moment the assertion was out of her mouth, Karla knew it was true; she might very well be soaring in a fool's paradise disguised to look like heaven, but until she was forced to vacate the state of euphoria, she felt equal to whatever it had to offer.

Barred during the fall season from the floor of the pastoral canyon, they viewed the scene from pullouts along the south rim drive. Karla felt thrilled as she stood near the edge of a sheer cliff. While staring several hundred feet down, she was enthralled by the sound of Jared's voice as he continued in his role of tour guide.

"As you can see," he said at one pullout, pointing to a scattering of dwellings on the canyon floor, "the canyon is inhabited—but not during the colder months. Most Navajo families abandon the canyon in the winter."

"Where do they go?" Karla asked abstractedly, as she stared in consternation at one particular section that was cut in half by the Río de Chelly.

"To their homes up here, along the rim." He paused, then asked, "What are you staring at?"

Karla slanted a smile at him, then returned her gaze to the tall cottonwood trees clustered on the banks of the river. "How odd," she mused. "I've never been here before, yet I recognize that section of the floor and the far canyon wall looming over it."

Jared laughed. "There's nothing at all odd about it. As a matter of fact, you admired that scene in my living room a few nights ago."

Memory clicked, and Karla glanced up at him in surprise. "The canyon painting above your fireplace!" she exclaimed. "You did that here?"

"From this very spot," Jared admitted, laughing at

her astonished expression. "I wondered if you'd noticed."

"How could I help but notice?" Karla demanded, shifting her gaze between him and the site. "You painted from the photographs you snapped while standing here ... Right?"

"Wrong."

Her eyes flew wide. "You painted it while standing this close to the edge of the rim?"

"Correct." Jared's strong teeth flashed in a grin.

"Have you no fear?"

The grin was wiped away by the seriousness of his expression. "I have many fears, Karla, but none of them are connected to heights in any way, shape, or form."

Naturally, Karla was intensely curious about the nature of Jared's fears. She was in love, truly in love, for the first time in her life, and like all lovers throughout history, she wanted to garner every scrap of information about her beloved. Questions collided into one another as they converged on her tongue. An alerted sense of caution held them at bay.

The relationship unfolding between her and Jared was still very tenuous; they had shared few confidences. Other than the question he had asked about her long period of celibacy, he had refrained from prying into her life. Karla was afraid to give in to the temptation to probe into his most personal feelings and emotions, for fear she might tip the delicate balance and turn him away from her. Choosing prudence, she refused the questions passage through her lips.

"Fortunately, I don't suffer from acrophobia, either," she finally said, turning from him to return to the car. "Where do we go from here?"

Jared replied in the literal sense, promising that from

the next overlook they would be able to see an Anasazi pueblo consisting of ten rooms and two kivas, or ceremonial rooms, on the far side of the canyon. He also promised her a peek into a real hogan, the traditional Navajo dwelling—which turned out to be a replica of the mound-shaped structures Karla had puzzled over the day before.

Though Karla was genuinely interested, and told him so, the metaphorical quality of her question—"Where do we go from here?"—taunted her at intervals throughout the day.

After eating lunch in the cafeteria at Thunderbird Lodge, they set out for Monument Valley. Karla filled the long driving hours by testing Jared's knowledge with a barrage of questions about the reservation.

Having no idea what to expect, Karla was suitably impressed by the enormous rock monuments in the valley—buttes, mesas, canyons, and free-standing rock formations in various hues ranging from pink to dark red.

The sun set in a blaze of magenta and violet as they ate dinner in a restaurant in the town of Kayenta, where Karla tasted Indian fried bread for the first time and declared it delicious.

Replete with good food, and pleasantly tired from their long day, they were content to listen to the taped music Jared slid into the deck as they drove through darkness to Wahweap Lodge and Marina at Lake Powell.

Since she couldn't see much of the lake, other than a few lights reflecting off the inky water, Karla was satisfied to follow Jared to their rooms without complaint after he checked them in at the desk.

As he had the night before, Jared opened the door for

her, set her suitcases inside the room, asked her if she was pleased with the accommodations, then left her. He walked back into her room, carrying wine and glasses, thirty minutes later.

The wine was delicious; their lovemaking was better.

The instant Jared drew her naked body to his, Karla knew their rite of union would be different. "Different" inadequately described it. His mouth was a scorching brand; his tongue a flickering torment. His restless hands made her wild with need; his hot, plundering body drove her over the edge of reason. And, when the tumult was over, he cradled her as if she were fashioned of delicate crystal.

Karla loved every minute of it.

That night, by mutual if unspoken consent, they set the pattern for the remainder of their trip.

Karla and Jared spent two thoroughly relaxing days at the lake, which revealed itself a sparkling sapphire in the glittering rays of the late fall sunlight.

From the side of a tour boat, Karla marveled at the huge, multishaped rocks rising like ancient monoliths from the 180-square-mile man-made lake. She stared in awed appreciation as the boat glided through some of the ninety-six canyon passages and sailed to within gasping distance of the impressive 583-foot-high arc of the Glen Canyon Dam.

Accustomed to a personal report from Jared, Karla was deaf to the droning voice of the tour guide, preferring the more exciting low tones of her lover.

"This is a newer addition to the modern West," Jared said. "The lake is named for John Wesley Powell, the geologist who charted the Colorado River. The dam cost 260 million dollars to construct, and was completed in the fall of 1963. Electrical sales of more than 350 million dollars have been produced since it opened in 1964."

Karla had been admiring the scene, not looking at him, but she glanced up with a dutifully respectful expression. "You must have a fantastic memory," she praised on a burst of laughter. "How in the world have you retained those dates and figures?"

To her amazement, Jared grinned rather sheepishly, and rustled a pamphlet he held in his hand. "It's all in this guidebook I picked up in the lodge."

The sound of Karla's delighted laughter rang out in the crisp air. An instant later, Jared's deeper laughter blended with hers. Their merging laughter set another pattern for the remainder of their jaunt.

From Lake `Powell they drove across the Arizona state line into Utah to yet another, quite different, canyon, this one named Bryce.

"About sixty million years old," Jared informed her dryly. This time he refrained from adding, "yet still an integral part of the modern West."

"I'm getting the picture," Karla retorted abstractedly, enchanted by cities of stone castles, temples, spires, and windowed walls in radiant shades of red, pink, and white below the plateau rim. "But," she went on as they turned away from the magnificent view, "I'm afraid I'm also beginning to get canyoned out . . . if you know what I mean?"

Jared chuckled, but nodded his understanding. "Only one more to go . . . at least for a while . . . and I think you'll find it a pleasant change."

Remembering that she had chosen to hear the itinerary on a day-to-day basis, Karla contained her curiosity and tamped down the urge to ask him exactly what he'd meant with his wryly inserted "at least for a while." But his final assertion proved correct.

After leaving Bryce Canyon they stopped for a late lunch, then drove directly to Zion National Park where, Karla was relieved to discover, tourists were required to view the massive stone edifices by craning their necks as they looked up from the canyon floor.

They spent the night wrapped in comfort, and each other's arms, in the deceptively rustic Zion Lodge. In the morning, Jared confused and intrigued Karla by allowing her to linger over her shower and subsequent breakfast, instead of rushing her through both in order to get an early start. When she queried him about his new attitude, Jared smiled mysteriously and gave her a brief answer.

"We don't have too far to drive to our next destination."

"And where might that be?" Karla asked.

"You'll see," he replied, slanting a rakish grin at her. "But brace yourself, after all this natural beauty, you might be in for mild cultural shock."

Las Vegas . . . cultural shock indeed. Glitz, glamour, hordes of people, from the narrow-eyed professional gambler to the wide-eyed tourist. The city's garish opulence clashed jarringly with the natural wonders Jared had shown Karla, yet it also was a very real, integral part of the modern West.

Karla hated it. After the sweeping beauty and freedom of nature's eerily silent solitude, the noise, the lights, and the crowds gave her a smothering, uneasy feeling of claustrophobia. And since Jared evinced not a shred of interest in contributing any of his money to the casinos, Karla didn't hesitate to inquire about the length of their visit.

"I booked the rooms for two nights," he replied, then satisfied her curiosity concerning the vague statement he'd made while they were at Bryce Canyon. "From here we go to Hoover Dam, then straight through to the main attraction."

"The Grand Canyon?" Karla asked, suffering conflicting feelings—anticipation of the most acclaimed of the Seven Wonders of the modern world, and reluctance to stand on yet another canyon rim so soon.

"Yes, the Grand," Jared confirmed. "The arrangements are made, but I can change them if you'd prefer to spend just one night here in Vegas."

"No," Karla said quickly. "We'll stick to the original schedule and stay two nights."

As it turned out, they were fated to stay only the one night in the city of blazing neon.

The room they were escorted to in the large casino hotel was decorated in Twentieth-Century Decadent style. By avoiding each other's eyes, Karla and Jared successfully contained their amusement until the bellboy finished fussing and departed, smiling in a superior way over the size of the tip Jared placed in his boldly outstretched hand. But their laughter exploded seconds after the door was shut with a gentle click.

"I feel positively immoral!" Karla gasped, choking on another burst of laughter.

"Yeah." Jared leered exaggeratedly. "Would you be open to the suggestion of a private orgy?" He wiggled his eyebrows at her. "I can call room service and order champagne and caviar."

Karla's responsive leer was as suggestive as his had been. "Why don't you do that? It sounds like fun."

It was.

While many of the hotel guests played games of

chance in the casino, Karla and Jared play games of a sensual nature on the enormous round bed in the suite he had taken in exchange for their two single rooms. Their loving play, begun with laughter, swiftly escalated into passionate intensity. They shared the caviar, the wine and their bodies with fervor and abandon, reveling in the joy and wonder of being together.

Strangely, it was in this artificial setting that Karla also abandoned her inner self to her lover.

"I was very young and very impressionable, and I believed myself very much in love," Karla said abruptly, staring at the ceiling.

They were lying side by side on the circular bed, replete and exhausted. Karla knew Jared was awake; his one hand was stroking her thigh soothingly. His hand stilled at the detached sound of her voice. She felt the mattress shift as he rolled onto his side to gaze down at her. A frown knitted his brow; concern darkened his eyes.

"The memory still hurts?"

Karla didn't look at him as she considered his question. Then, at the realization that she felt nothing—not a lingering shred of pain, humiliation, or remorse—she turned her head on the pillow and smiled at him.

"No. I think I've finally outgrown the effects." Satisfaction shimmered through her as she caught the faint sound of his relieved sigh.

"Do you want to tell me about it? . . . about him?"

Her smile slanted wryly. "There's not much to tell, about either it or him. And there's certainly nothing new about the story." She managed a shrug. "I was an afterthought. My parents were middle-aged when I was born. Their only other child, my sister, was fifteen, and they were all less than thrilled with the demands of an infant. When I met him"—Karla never mentioned *him* by name; Jared didn't ask—"I was a freshman in college, and starved for love and affection. He was more than happy to provide both, for a price."

"A price!" Jared exclaimed, sitting up suddenly. "What sort of price?"

Warmth spread through Karla at the scowl of outrage on his handsome face. She blinked against a sting in her eyes and swallowed to clear her throat. "My independence, my freedom, and my studies," she answered tightly. "I quit school to support him, I devoted my life to him, and in exchange he told me he loved me . . . oh, at least once a week, whether I needed to hear it or not. When I realized I didn't need it, or him, I left."

"The bastard used you shamelessly," he snarled.

"Yes," she agreed calmly. "But if I haven't learned anything else, I've learned one truth."

"And that is . . . ?"

"The only way one person can use another is with the other's consent." Recalling Anne's description of Jared as a user, Karla looked him straight in the eyes. "I will never consent again, Jared," she said in a cool, steady tone.

Jared's eyes flashed with anger. "Are you accusing me of having used you this past week?" he demanded.

"No." As she made the denial, Karla lifted her hand to smooth the scowl from his face. "I'm saying I understand that, for now, and with mutual consent, we are using each other." Curling her hand around the back of his neck, she drew his head down to hers.

"Karla . . ."

She flicked her tongue over his mouth. "I'm tired of talking," she whispered. "Why don't you shut up and use me some more?"

Jared didn't have to be coaxed. But before he succumbed to the headiness of passion, he made her a promise . . . a promise that had the sound of a threat.

"We will talk about this tomorrow. I think there are a few more blank spaces that need to be filled in."

But they didn't have the discussion. Their sight-seeing jaunt came to a jarring end with the shrill ring of the telephone early the next morning.

CHAPTER TEN

THE RENTAL CAR Jared had arranged for was waiting for
them when they landed in Phoenix. Her mind whirling
in reaction to the swiftness of events, Karla followed in
his wake like an automaton. There had been little time
for discussion, or even for rational thought. Jared's
command had been "Move!" and, repressing the questions that had flooded her mind, Karla had rushed to
obey; his harsh tone of voice precluded any other response.

But once they were inside the privacy of their car on
the last leg of their journey home, with Jared maintaining his stoic silence, Karla had time to recollect her
whirling thoughts and reflect on the reason for their pre-
cipitous flight.

It hurt like hell, but there was one fact of which
Karla was certain: Their tryst, or affair, or whatever it

had been, was over, ended by that pre-dawn phone call. Fighting tears and an overwhelming need to scream in protest, she avoided looking at Jared's rigidly set profile by staring out of the side window at the sun-splashed scenery racing by. Trying to bring her thoughts into a semblance of order, she recalled the events since he had answered the phone.

She had been hazy and only half awake when she'd heard Jared speaking softly. The sudden change in his voice from sleepy relaxation to alert tautness had dispersed the haziness, jolting her into full wakefulness. Karla had registered little of his side of the brief conversation, other than the terseness of his replies. When he cradled the receiver and turned to her, she had found herself staring at a stranger.

"We've got to leave," he'd said flatly, giving her neither explanation nor option.

"What?" Scraping her tousled hair back from her face, Karla had struggled to free herself from the tangled covers and sit up. "Why? What's wrong?"

Headed for the bathroom, Jared had paused to give her a bleak look and an abrupt answer. "I must get back to Sedona. My father's dying." His expression didn't change with her shocked gasp. "I'd appreciate your help," he went on in a tone that belonged to the stranger he'd become. "While I shower will you call the desk and ask the clerk to prepare the bill?"

"Yes, of course, but—" That was as far as he'd allowed her to go.

"Later, Karla, please," he'd interrupted impatiently, turning away to stride into the bathroom.

Later never came; there was neither time nor the proper circumstances. Before she stepped into the shower, Karla heard him speaking rapidly into the phone.

By the time she was bathed, dressed, and packed, he had completed his arrangements and was waiting at the door, his body taut with the need for action.

Though concluded swiftly, Jared's arrangements were comprehensive. His car was left at the parking garage near the airport. Seats had been secured for them on an early morning flight out of Vegas. A rental car would be waiting for them on their arrival in Phoenix.

Jared's plans fell into sequence like clockwork. There was only one thing missing—the time or opportunity for any clarifying explanations. He informed her that the call had come from his father's physician advising him to return to Sedona as quickly as possible, and he outlined his arrangements, but beyond that, Jared had offered her no further enlightenment, least of all on his emotional state.

Karla had been left to flounder in the dark with her guesswork. Without any information from Jared to guide her, the answers she was arriving at were far from reassuring. She felt deserted, bereft, deprived of warmth.

As they approached the environs of Sedona, Jared broke the silence, shattering her brooding introspection with a startling request. "Will you wait at my place for me?"

Wait? His place? The question fragments sparked a physical response. Turning around in her seat, Karla stared at him in blank astonishment.

"Jared, I don't understand." She shook her head as if to clear the cobwebs from her mind. "You have told me absolutely nothing! What is it you want me to wait for?"

"For me," he answered, glancing at her. His expression comprised a mixture of regret and appeal. "I know I haven't explained and I'm sorry, but there just wasn't time." He returned his gaze to the road, presenting to her a profile that was no longer harsh and forbidding; the stranger was gone, Jared was back. "And there still isn't any time," he added. "I'll have to leave for the hospital as soon as I've dropped you off, but I promise I'll explain everything to you when I get home." He had to stop for a red light, and turned to her again. "Will you wait there for me?"

They were at a crossroad, figuratively as well as literally. Karla had the feeling that their relationship hinged on her answer; she knew that contingent to her response, Jared would either turn left to her apartment or right to his house.

When the traffic light flicked to green, Karla told him to turn right, and felt a deep sense of gratification tremble through her at the spasm of relief that was fleetingly revealed in his eyes and expression.

His brief display of emotion kept Karla bound to his house during the ensuing hours of waiting and wondering. Taking only enough time to carry their suitcases into the house, tell her to make herself at home, and kiss her hard but quickly in passing, Jared was gone, leaving her with her fears and speculations.

In consequence, it was a very long day, and an even longer night, for Karla. In an attempt to avoid conjecture, she employed herself with busywork, changing into jeans, a loose pullover top, and flat-heeled shoes before exploring the house, unpacking Jared's and her own suitcases, and then carrying their soiled clothes to the laundry room. While the clothing swished back and forth in the washer, Karla made lunch, consisting of a sandwich, which she didn't finish, and a pot of coffee, which she polished off completely. After switching the clean clothing to the dryer, she dusted every piece of furniture and vacuumed every floor in the house. When the dryer shut off, she folded the clothes and piled them neatly on Jared's bed. Occasionally—like every two or three minutes—she glanced first at the clock, then at the phone. The hands on the clock continued to move at a crawl. The bell inside the phone remained silent. And it was that nerve-racking silence that finally drove her from the house.

While exploring the uneven terrain around the house, Karla discovered a narrow path. Deciding to investigate, she followed the switchback trail to the base of the jutting overhang on which the building had been constructed. The path led to an open area that sloped gently down to the gurgling Oak Creek. Tall trees, still in leaf, stood sentinel along the creek banks, their leaves shimmering in the sunlight and whispering sighs in the light breeze.

Dropping to the ground in the dappled shade, Karla stared at the water tripping over the rocks in the creek bed, and surrendered to the questions running through her mind. Set free, the questions condensed into one all-encompassing thought.

Where did they go from here?

Karla was half afraid to even consider the probabilities. After nearly a week spent exclusively in Jared's company, she had grown accustomed to, and almost comfortable with, the realization of the deep love she felt for him. And though she wouldn't have believed it possible mere days before, she was ready to make a commitment to Jared.

Jared.

Karla sighed as his name whispered with aching longing through her mind. She was irrevocably in love with him and yearned to admit it to him and to the entire world. Yet, through all their days of lighthearted sightseeing and all their nights of shared sensuous pleasure, she had bitten back the words of love that had trembled to her lips, waiting, hoping first to hear encouraging words from him.

Her wait had been in vain. Except for that one impassioned moment when he had said he loved her in retaliation for her glib remark about being "in lust," Jared had not mentioned love again. Karla's biggest fear was that he might never say those precious words again.

Against her desire and will, an echo of Anne's voice rang persistently in Karla's mind. Jared the ruthless; Jared the user. The accusations revolved in ever widening circles inside her head. Anne's description of Jared was completely contradictory to Karla's own observations of him. Either Anne or she was wrong. But which one?

Motivated by his admitted desire for her, had Jared deliberately, ruthlessly assumed a persona that he believed would appeal to her?

The question kept Karla awake most of that night. Only Jared himself could give her the answers she so desperately needed, and she hadn't heard a word from him since he'd rushed to the hospital that morning.

Alone in the pre-dawn darkness, feeling small and lost in Jared's king-size bed, Karla gave way to the tears stinging her gritty eyes. Crying softly, she drifted into a light, uneasy slumber.

"Karla."

Jared's quiet voice awoke her mind; his gentle touch aroused her senses. A faint smile feathered her lips as she whispered his name. Then memory stirred. Springing upright, she searched his face with alarm-widened eyes. He looked utterly exhausted. His eyes were dull with weariness; his face had an ashen pallor; deep grooves bracketed his mouth. Karla had to force herself to ask what had to be asked.

"Your father?"

"He's alive." Sighing heavily, Jared sank onto the bed beside her. It was only then that Karla realized he was naked. She opened her mouth to question him; he silenced her with a plea she was helpless to refuse. "Not now, Karla, please. I need you so much, and I need you now. I'm so tired. I'm freezing. I need to be inside the warmth of your arms, your body. Karla, give me your warmth. Help me rest."

In answer to his plea, Karla held out her arms in invitation and unconditional surrender. She loved him; she could not deny him the physical expression of that love.

Jared made love to Karla like a man driven by inner demons. There was a wildness riding him that ignited a corresponding frenzy in her. His hot mouth seared hers, crushing her soft lips while inflicting exquisite pleasure; she heightened the sensation by sinking her teeth into his lips and tongue. His hands didn't caress, they grasped her flesh possessively; she gasped, but spurred him on with whimpering moans of encouragement. When his hands roughly parted her thighs, she arched her hips in a brazen demand for his invasion. And when at last he thrust his body into the depths of her silken warmth, she threw back her head, crying aloud for more.

Their combined furor produced the most incredible simultaneous release imaginable.

Feeling shattered and nearly insensible, Karla forced her heavy eyelids open when Jared moved away from her. Her eyes widened in shock at the sight of him. His face was a twisted mask of anguished shame and self-disgust. Without a murmur, he turned away from her, sprawled across the bed on his stomach, and immediately fell asleep.

Sleep was not in the cards for Karla. Dragging her aching body from the bed, she stumbled to the bathroom, then stood beneath a stinging shower, unmindful of the hot tears that mingled with the pounding spray that sluiced over her face and body. She stood under the beating water until it ran cold.

Feeling partially revived and almost human after her shower, Karla dressed, then wandered into the kitchen to brew a pot of coffee. It was to be the first in a day that overflowed with pots of coffee. Cup in hand, as if it had attached itself to her palm, Karla spent most of the day drifting aimlessly about the house and its immediate surroundings. She needed sleep, but her body refused to rest; she needed to think, but her mind refused to function.

In midafternoon, cradling yet another freshly brewed cup of coffee in her hands, Karla trailed listlessly down the path to the creek bank. Sitting cross-legged, she rested her back against the tree trunk and stared into the shallow water, intermittently sipping at the coffee. She had no idea how long she'd been sitting there when she felt rather than heard Jared sit down next to her.

"I'm sorry."

Karla shut her eyes in acceptance of the tremor of pain and remorse that shook her body. Two tears escaped to slide slowly down her pale cheeks. Her eyes flew open when she felt him move and heard him murmur her name in a deep, agonized groan.

"Karla, don't cry." He was on his knees beside her. With trembling hands, he took the cup from her and set it to one side, then gently drew her into his arms. "I love you, and now I've hurt you. And after swearing I'd die before I hurt you." A shudder tore through the length of his body. "I'm no better than my father ever was."

His vow of love for her sank to Karla's soul; his cry of self-condemnation speared to the heart of her compassion. She leaned back to stare into his face. "No better?" she repeated, confused. "Jared, I don't understand."

"I know." He released her and sat straight. A faint, bitter smile curved his mouth. "That night when you were . . ." He paused and his smile turned wry. "Should I say you were wary, if not really afraid of me?"

Karla's smile was as wry as his; she still wasn't about to admit to being more afraid of her own feelings than of him. "What about that night?"

Jared's smile faded. "At some point between that morning and that night, you heard the local gossip about me, all the gory details about how cruelly and ruthlessly I had treated my father . . . didn't you?"

"Yes." Karla swallowed, then blurted out, "I was also told that you were ruthless in your use of women."

His spine stiffened. "That's not true." His voice was strong and held the solid ring of sincerity. "I admit to being harsh with my father, but I have never misused any woman. And I'm certain that, if asked, every woman I was ever involved with would tell you the same. The affairs were always conducted on equal terms, to mutual satisfaction."

Karla suppressed a shiver. "It sounds very business-like and impersonal," she said, unable to suppress her vivid memories of the intensely personal, yet warmly friendly, relationship they'd shared the previous week.

"I scrupulously kept my alliances impersonal," he replied, "in self-defense. You see, Karla, I was rigid in my determination never to enslave myself to a woman by falling in love with her, the way my mother allowed her love to chain her to my father."

His father! Karla suddenly understood that key to Jared's character had to do with his relationship with his father. And with sudden clarity she could see his vulnerability. "Do you hate your father that much?" she asked softly.

Jared sighed. "If any man deserved to be hated, he did."

"What did he do to earn your hatred?" she asked, knowing intuitively that he did not hate lightly or easily.

"It's a long story and not a very pretty one," Jared said wearily.

"I'm not in a hurry to go anywhere." Karla tried a tentative smile, and felt heartened when he smiled back at her.

"All right," he relented. "I'll condense it, give you the salient points." He narrowed his eyes, whether against the long rays of the setting sun or in concentration, she had no way of knowing; Karla only knew that the warmth was leaving the day, but slowly creeping back into her body.

"Like many of his contemporaries, my father grew to manhood disliking Indians, and so, as you can imagine, he was torn with inner conflict when he fell in love with my mother, the daughter of a man he sneeringly referred to as 'the half-breed' and who just happened to be the best cattleman his father had ever employed. But, indulged by a wealthy father, and accustomed to having what he wanted, my father married my mother, then proceeded to make life damned near impossible for her.

Her father lived on the ranch in a trailer parked in the tiny section of land my father's father deeded over to him before he died. That transaction only deepened my father's hate. When he was at home, he forbade my mother to visit her father. Fortunately, he was away on business a lot.

"I adored both my mother and my grandfather, and my father knew it, which didn't exactly endear me to him." Jared shrugged. "Hell, I had two strikes against me with him from the day I was born, simply because I was the spit and image of my grandfather"—he sliced a dry smile at her—"as you noticed the first time we met at the gallery."

The large painting flashed into Karla's mind. She smiled and nodded.

"My father made life a living hell for my mother, my grandfather, and me," Jared continued grimly. "When I got old enough to take care of her, I urged my mother to leave him to his hate and bitterness. She refused. When I asked why, she explained very simply that she loved him. She was such a beautiful, gentle woman, and yet she stayed with him, accepting all the hell he dished out to her, simply because she loved him." A muscle twitched in his jaw. "I didn't share her feelings, but I continued to live at home to protect her. The day she was buried I walked away from his house and his hate."

"Then your father suffered a stroke," she said softly, "and you refused to go see him."

The wry smile reappeared. "And earned a reputation for being ruthless. That was a few years ago. The reputation has grown with each passing year and with every crisis I've ignored."

Karla frowned. "Yet this time when he called for you, you went to him. Why?"

Jared's expression sent hope soaring through her veins. "Because of you . . . and something you said."

"You went because of me!" she exclaimed. "But, Jared, I didn't say a word! You didn't ask for my opinion."

He shook his head. "You didn't have to say anything. You were there, sharing my bed, laughing with me, healing me."

"Oh, Jared." Karla could say no more for the emotional tears clogging her throat.

"It was touch and go for a long time there at the hospital, Karla." His expression looked haunted. "He didn't recognize me when I arrived, and I sat beside him waiting . . . waiting. I hadn't the vaguest idea what I'd say to him if he did recognize me, but"—he drew a rough breath—"sometime during the night he had an attack or something. I had to leave the room while the doctors worked on him. They have him in one of those constant-care rooms—you know, the kind that are all windows?" He arched his brows and when she nodded, continued, "I stood at that window, watching him fight for his life, remembering what you had said about consent. And I was forced to realize that my mother had a choice. He loved her obsessively, and hated her because of it. But he could never have used her without her consent. When the doctors left his room, they looked at me in confused wonder; that old man had confounded them again by surviving yet another crisis. He was lucid and knew me. I made my peace with him, Karla. I'll never like him, but I no longer hate him. I guess that's something."

"No, Jared," she corrected softly, "that's a great deal."

He was quiet for a while. Then, raising his hand, he

touched her hair. "I like your hair down the way you've been wearing it . . . Did I tell you?"

"Yes." Karla's heart melted. "Every time we made love."

His hand went still; his voice went low, and held an unfamiliar uncertain tone. "I was pretty rough with you this morning. I have no excuse, except that I needed you so badly, I lost control, and that has never happened to me before."

She reached out to stroke the tension from his face. "I understand."

"But I used you!"

She arched her eyebrows.

Jared laughed. "With your consent?"

She laughed with him. "Of course."

His eyes began to glitter in the way that never failed to excite her. Then he drew her into his embrace. "Are you still in lust with me, Karla?" he asked in a rough-edged whisper.

"No."

Jared's body grew taut, and he shifted around until she was flat on her back and he was arching over her. "No?" he repeated in a growled demand. "How can you say that after the way we made love this morning? Dammit, Karla. Answer me!"

"Are you still in love with me?" she answered with a demand of her own.

"Yes! I love you!" he growled. "Now, tell me, why aren't you still in lust with me?"

Karla's smile was serene. "Because I'm in love with you . . . and lust and love are two entirely different things."

Jared's laughter began as a low rumble that quickly built into a joyous roar. "You know, you're right. I guess I have been in lust before, and there's no compari-

son. Lust isn't bad," he conceded, swooping down to
kiss her fiercely. "But love's a lot better."

"I know."

And there, lying in the last golden rays of sunshine,
they proceeded to prove their point.

And as her wedding gift to him, Karla sent Jared the
portrait of his grandfather.

SECOND CHANCE AT LOVE

COMING NEXT MONTH

FOUL PLAY #456
by Steffie Hall
Handsome veterinarian Jake Elliott
has already rescued Amy Klasse once; now
her reputation's at stake. Will Jake
be able to save it—and their
newfound love, too?

THE RIALTO AFFAIR #457
by Jan Mathews
Two years ago, Dr. Amanda Pearson
gave criminal lawyer Tyler Marshall more
than the professional testimony he needed to
win his case. Amanda had given herself,
too. Now Ty's back—and he won't
let her defense rest.

Second Chance At Love

BE SURE TO READ...

ALL THE FLOWERS #452
by Mary Modean
Though they've been apart for years,
time has only increased the love
Joanna McKenna still feels for her
ex-husband, Jerrod. But so much else
has changed...Maybe just enough
so that Joanna can go home again.

BLONDES PREFER GENTLEMEN #453
by Diana Morgan
James William Bentley is intrigued,
to say the least, when he sees Susan
Melinka, a beautiful stowaway on board
this luxury liner, stealing champagne
from under his nose. Will love at first
sight be threatened when sudden on-board
hints of more serious thefts abound?

Order on opposite page

SECOND CHANCE AT LOVE

___ 0-425-10225-4	TWO'S COMPANY #412 Sherryl Woods	$2.25
___ 0-425-10226-2	WINTER FLAME #413 Kelly Adams	$2.25
___ 0-425-10227-0	A SWEET TALKIN' MAN #414 Jackie Leigh	$2.25
___ 0-425-10228-9	TOUCH OF MIDNIGHT #415 Kerry Price	$2.25
___ 0-425-10229-7	HART'S DESIRE #416 Linda Raye	$2.25
___ 0-425-10230-0	A FAMILY AFFAIR #417 Cindy Victor	$2.25
___ 0-425-10513-X	CUPID'S CAMPAIGN #418 Kate Gilbert	$2.50
___ 0-425-10514-8	GAMBLER'S LADY #419 Cait Logan	$2.50
___ 0-425-10515-6	ACCENT ON DESIRE #420 Christa Merlin	$2.50
___ 0-425-10516-4	YOUNG AT HEART #421 Jackie Leigh	$2.50
___ 0-425-10517-2	STRANGER FROM THE PAST #422 Jan Mathews	$2.50
___ 0-425-10518-0	HEAVEN SENT #423 Jamisan Whitney	$2.50
___ 0-425-10530-X	ALL THAT JAZZ #424 Carole Buck	$2.50
___ 0-425-10531-8	IT STARTED WITH A KISS #425 Kit Windham	$2.50
___ 0-425-10558-X	ONE FROM THE HEART #426 Cinda Richards	$2.50
___ 0-425-10559-8	NIGHTS IN SHINING SPLENDOR #427 Christina Dair	$2.50
___ 0-425-10560-1	ANGEL ON MY SHOULDER #428 Jackie Leigh	$2.50
___ 0-425-10561-X	RULES OF THE HEART #429 Samantha Quinn	$2.50
___ 0-425-10604-7	PRINCE CHARMING REPLIES #430 Sherryl Woods	$2.50
___ 0-425-10605-5	DESIRE'S DESTINY #431 Jamisan Whitney	$2.50
___ 0-425-10680-2	A LADY'S CHOICE #432 Cait Logan	$2.50
___ 0-425-10681-0	CLOSE SCRUTINY #433 Pat Dalton	$2.50
___ 0-425-10682-9	SURRENDER THE DAWN #434 Jan Mathews	$2.50
___ 0-425-10683-7	A WARM DECEMBER #435 Jacqueline Topaz	$2.50
___ 0-425-10708-6	RAINBOW'S END #436 Carole Buck	$2.50
___ 0-425-10709-4	TEMPTRESS #437 Linda Raye	$2.50
___ 0-425-10743-4	CODY'S GYPSY #438 Courtney Ryan	$2.50
___ 0-425-10744-2	THE LADY EVE #439 Dana Daniels	$2.50
___ 0-425-10836-8	RELEASED INTO DAWN #440 Kelly Adams	$2.50
___ 0-425-10837-6	STAR LIGHT, STAR BRIGHT #441 Frances West	$2.50
___ 0-425-10873-2	A LADY'S DESIRE #442 Cait Logan	$2.50
___ 0-425-10874-0	ROMANCING CHARLEY #443 Hilary Cole	$2.50
___ 0-425-10914-3	STRANGER THAN FICTION #444 Diana Morgan	$2.50
___ 0-425-10915-1	FRIENDLY PERSUASION #445 Laine Allen	$2.50
___ 0-425-10945-3	KNAVE OF HEARTS #446 Jasmine Craig	$2.50
___ 0-425-10946-1	TWO FOR THE ROAD #447 Kit Windham	$2.50
___ 0-425-10986-0	THE REAL THING #448 Carole Buck	$2.50
___ 0-425-10987-9	SOME KIND OF WONDERFUL #449 Adrienne Edwards	$2.50

Please send the titles I've checked above. Mail orders to:

BERKLEY PUBLISHING GROUP
390 Murray Hill Pkwy., Dept B
East Rutherford, NJ 07073

NAME _____

ADDRESS _____

CITY _____

STATE _____ ZIP _____

Please allow 6 weeks for delivery.
Prices are subject to change without notice.

POSTAGE & HANDLING:
$1.00 for one book, $.25 for each
additional. Do not exceed $3.50.

BOOK TOTAL	$____
SHIPPING & HANDLING	$____
APPLICABLE SALES TAX (CA, NJ, NY, PA)	$____
TOTAL AMOUNT DUE	$____
PAYABLE IN US FUNDS. (No cash orders accepted.)